"Are you all right, Ms

"Yes, it was just a scary night." Peyton's gaze met Liam's. "I understand your father died that night saving others. I'm sorry."

"He did lose his life that night, along with others. If there's anything else you can tell me, I need you to speak up."

"I wish I could tell you who set that fire, but I honestly don't know."

"I reviewed my father's notes on the investigation into Inman's claims. According to Inman's statement, he overheard you saying someone on staff gave Mrs. Inman the wrong medication."

Peyton tried to control her temper. This wasn't a chat. It was an interrogation.

"But you denied making such a statement."

"That's correct."

"Why would he say that if it wasn't true?"

"I answered that before. He was distraught and desperate to blame someone."

"So, you stand by your original statement, that you don't believe the hospital was responsible?"

"I do." She heaved another breath. "Now, can I go? I need to check on my mother."

"Yes, for now."

SUSPICIOUS CIRCUMSTANCES

USA TODAY Bestselling Author

RITA HERRON

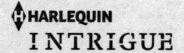

HARLEQUIN
INTRIGUE

To all the nurses in the world; you're the real heroes.

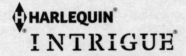

INTRIGUE

ISBN-13: 978-1-335-13675-6

Recycling programs
for this product may
not exist in your area.

Suspicious Circumstances

Copyright © 2020 by Rita B. Herron

This edition published by arrangement with Harlequin Books S.A.

For questions and comments about the quality of this book,
please contact us at CustomerService@Harlequin.com.

Harlequin Enterprises ULC
22 Adelaide St. West, 40th Floor
Toronto, Ontario M5H 4E3, Canada
www.Harlequin.com

Printed in U.S.A.

USA TODAY bestselling author **Rita Herron** wrote her first book when she was twelve but didn't think real people grew up to be writers. Now she writes so she doesn't have to get a real job. A former kindergarten teacher and workshop leader, she traded storytelling to kids for writing romance, and now she writes romantic comedies and romantic suspense. Rita lives in Georgia with her family. She loves to hear from readers, so please visit her website, ritaherron.com.

Books by Rita Herron

Harlequin Intrigue

A Badge of Honor Mystery

Mysterious Abduction
Left to Die
Protective Order
Suspicious Circumstances

Badge of Justice

Redemption at Hawk's Landing
Safe at Hawk's Landing
Hideaway at Hawk's Landing
Hostage at Hawk's Landing

The Heroes of Horseshoe Creek

Lock, Stock and McCullen
McCullen's Secret Son
Roping Ray McCullen
Warrior Son
The Missing McCullen
The Last McCullen

Cold Case at Camden Crossing
Cold Case at Carlton's Canyon
Cold Case at Cobra Creek
Cold Case in Cherokee Crossing

Visit the Author Profile page at Harlequin.com.

CAST OF CHARACTERS

Special Agent Liam Maverick—He will do anything to find his father's killer.

Nurse Peyton Weiss—Will her secret get her killed?

Val Weiss—Why has Peyton's sister, who is addicted to drugs, resurfaced in her life?

Dr. Butler—He has incriminating documents against Peyton.

Joanna Horton—Peyton's best friend is the only one she trusts.

Herbert Brantley—Did he take money to hide the truth about Gloria Inman's death and the hospital fire?

Miller Conrad—Is he an angel of mercy?

Director Richard Jameson—Did he give Peyton her job to help her, or to keep tabs on her so she didn't talk?

Prologue

The hospital was on fire.

Screams of terror and panic filled the air. Firefighters and first responders rushed in to extinguish the blaze and assist the sick and helpless from the burning building to safety. They'd been working for half an hour now, ever since the alarm had sounded.

Nurse Peyton Weiss helped clear the last patient from the ER. "Come on, sweetie," she said as she helped an elderly woman into a wheelchair. "We have to move."

The little woman was crying and confused, gnarled hands shaking as she gripped the wheelchair, but Peyton murmured assurances to her as she steered the wheelchair out the emergency exit. The lawn was covered in patients, panicked family members, the hospital staff and now the press, and was virtually a minefield of terrified and injured people.

Heart hammering, she left the woman with a medic and scanned the chaos for her own mother. Margaret Weiss had been admitted with pneumonia a week ago.

The same day Barry Inman's wife had died in the ER.

Fear squeezed at Peyton's lungs as she raced across

the grassy lawn, searching beds, wheelchairs and stretchers. Though the hospital had tried to evacuate in an orderly fashion by floors and departments, order had deteriorated as the blaze rapidly spread.

Thick plumes of smoke made her eyes water, or maybe it was tears. There were casualties. Two burn victims already.

Some woman was screaming hysterically that she couldn't find her baby.

She stepped aside as a firefighter carried a man toward the triage area.

What if her mother hadn't made it out alive? Smoke inhalation was dangerous, especially in a patient with pneumonia.

She passed a group of portable beds where the medics and doctors were assessing and treating patients. Commotion from across the lawn jolted her, and she spotted a doctor starting CPR on a patient. She broke into a run. The patient was her mother. The attending physician, Dr. Butler.

"Mama!" She took her mother's hand. "Please, hang on."

"We're doing everything we can," Dr. Butler murmured as he continued compressions.

A sob welled in her throat. Seconds ticked by. She worked in the ER, dealt with life-and-death situations every day. But this patient was her own flesh and blood. The only family she had left. She couldn't lose her.

Everything that had happened the past week crashed back. The day Inman's wife died in the ER. Something had gone wrong. Peyton voiced her concerns to Dr. Butler. But he'd told her to keep quiet or her career would be in jeopardy.

She had medical bills to pay for her mother's care. Still, it was wrong, and they'd argued. That night when she'd gotten home, she'd received a threatening phone call.

Keep your mouth shut or your mother will end up like Gloria Inman.

She shuddered at the memory. Not the doctor's voice. But whose? She'd been angry. Scared. And terrified for her mother.

Her mother's body jerked. She gasped, then a breath.

"It's okay, Mama. You're going to make it." *Then we're moving away from Whistler.*

She'd done what the doctor ordered. Told the police she didn't know what had happened in the ER with Inman's wife.

But every night the truth haunted her. She was covering a mistake, one she feared had caused a woman's death.

And every day the lie she'd told hacked away at her conscience.

Chapter One

Five years later

Special Agent Liam Maverick braced his Glock at the ready as he crawled through the bushes toward the abandoned cabin where his prime suspect was holed up.

Five years ago, Barry Inman, husband of Gloria Inman who'd died in the ER at Whistler Hospital, had filed a lawsuit against the doctors claiming his wife died under suspicious circumstances. When the case had been thrown out of court, Inman threatened revenge.

The next day a horrific fire broke out at the hospital, destroyed countless lives and tore the town apart. Liam's own father, sheriff at the time, lost his life trying to save others.

His father was a hero. But he was gone. As they'd stood over their father's grave, he and his three brothers, Jacob, Fletch and Griff, vowed to find the culprit who'd started the blaze and make him pay.

The sense that he was finally going to accomplish that spurred his adrenaline, and he flattened his body until he was on his belly. Barbed wire tugged at his leather jacket as Liam inched beneath the fencing, but he used his gloved hand to push it back.

A few feet away, already perched between a cluster of trees on a hill, Fletch, who worked SAR on the Appalachian Trail under FEMA, aimed binoculars toward the house.

Recently, Fletch had found evidence in a cave where the man had been hiding, then began a full-fledged hunt for Inman in the mountains. Two days ago, he'd stumbled on footprints near an AT shelter and he'd tracked him to this isolated cabin. As they'd discussed, Fletch was not to try to take down the man himself. So, he'd called Liam and their brother Jacob, Whistler's sheriff, and given them the GPS coordinates, and here they were.

Fletch pointed toward the rickety porch, then mouthed confirmation that Inman was in the house. Liam gestured for Fletch to hold back. He and Jacob were armed and would approach.

About seventy feet ahead of him, Jacob had slipped past the fence and gestured to move ahead. Liam lifted himself off the ground, then crouched low as he and Jacob wove between thick trees and bushes. The weathered little house sat on top of a ridge, offering a view of anyone who might approach from the driveway and graveled road.

Not wanting to alert Inman, he and Jacob had parked a mile down the road, then hiked through the woods. Dusk was setting, and a gusty breeze picked up, rattling tree branches and tossing debris across the pine needles and withered grass in the backyard. An old tire swing swayed back and forth as the wind battered it, and a stray cat clawed at a trash bag that had been dumped at the side of the house.

Liam and Jacob crept closer, then divided. Jacob

headed around front while Liam checked the back door, then eased around to the side porch. A noise sounded just as he neared the broken window, and he paused and stayed behind the corner of the house.

Seconds ticked by. The wind whistled. The stray screeched and chased a chipmunk into the woods. The door to the side porch squeaked open.

Liam inched around the corner, aimed his gun and waited. A minute passed. Two. Then Inman poked his head out and looked around. The man looked a decade older. His once short hair was now long and shaggy. A foot-long raggedy beard hung down his chest to a point. And his clothes were ratty and dirty, the jacket he wore oversize and baggy on his bony frame.

He peered toward the right, then glanced to where Liam was hiding. His father's lifeless face as he'd said goodbye to him before the funeral flashed behind Liam's eyes.

If this man was responsible, he had to pay. Suffer.

The need for revenge ate at him, and he moved his finger to the trigger.

But his father's voice taunted him from the heavens. His father whose mantra had been *Respect and Protect*.

Liam gritted his teeth. He'd become an agent to honor his father.

He exhaled, then stepped from the shadows. "FBI. Hold it right there."

Inman's eyes looked glassy and wide with panic. A dilapidated pickup was parked beneath a makeshift carport. A heartbeat later, he took off running toward the truck.

"Stop or I'll shoot!" Liam yelled.

But Inman didn't halt. Instead he darted toward the

truck. Liam broke into a run just as Jacob yelled out a warning.

Determined to stop Inman, Liam fired a shot into the ground, but Inman snatched a shovel from the carport and swung it up in defense.

"You're not going to get away," Liam said as he moved closer. "It's over, Inman."

"We just want to talk," Jacob shouted.

Inman shook his head. "No, you don't. You want to pin that fire on me. And I didn't do it."

All guilty men claimed they were innocent. "Put the shovel down," Liam said as he inched closer.

"I'm not going to prison for something I didn't do," Inman bellowed.

"Then talk to us and help us find out who did set that fire," Liam said.

Jacob crept toward them, his gun trained on Inman, but Liam was closer. "Just put down the shovel."

Inman's eyes were wild, sweat pouring down his face. Then he threw the shovel at Liam and yanked open the door of the truck. Liam dodged the shovel, then lunged toward Inman. Inman fumbled with the key and tried to start the engine. Liam reached for his arm, but Inman swung the door to close it and slammed Liam's shoulder in the process.

Pain shot through Liam's arm, but he jerked the door open again, dragged the man from the truck and threw him to the ground.

Furious, he jammed the barrel of his weapon in Inman's face.

"Try that again and you're dead," Liam growled. He kept his gun on him while Jacob bent and handcuffed the bastard.

PEYTON'S HEART HAMMERED as she watched the evening news in the staff break room at Golden Gardens, the assisted-living and nursing home where she worked. After she'd left Whistler, she'd accepted a job at the facility to watch over her mother and had been looking over her shoulder ever since.

The words *Late Breaking News* scrolled across the TV screen, then the reporter spoke. "Special Agent Liam Maverick and Sheriff Jacob Maverick of Whistler made an arrest today in the case of the hospital fire that killed several people five years ago." A photograph of a thin man with a long beard flashed on-screen. "The person of interest, Barry Inman, a man who filed a lawsuit against Whistler Hospital, has been taken into custody. Inman made allegations that his wife's death was caused by negligence, but the day before the fire, the case was thrown out."

Footage of the fire as it engulfed the hospital, then the chaos on the lawn that followed, filled the screen.

Barry Inman looked weathered and defeated, a shell of the man who'd stood by his wife's bedside pleading for the doctors to save her. His devotion to his wife, Gloria, had been intense. His anger over her death a force to reckon with. And understandable.

Guilt pressed against Peyton's chest. So many lives had been destroyed that night.

Had Barry set the hospital on fire?

The threatening message she'd received about Gloria Inman's death played through her mind. Whoever had called her wanted to cover up the mistake.

Did Dr. Butler have something to do with the threat?

That was hard to believe. He was her mentor when she first came to Whistler. He seemed caring and conscientious. Did he really believe she'd made a mistake and he wanted to protect her career? Or was he covering for someone else?

The fire had started near the record room for the ER. The room where files were kept on all the patients. Evidence that could have proven Inman was right had disintegrated into ashes in that inferno.

Suspicions that had dogged her for years mounted again.

Then fear. If the person who'd threatened her saw that Inman had been arrested, he might think she'd talked.

Pulse pounding, she grabbed her purse from her locker and rushed from the room. She had to check on her mother.

Keeping her safe was the only thing that mattered.

LIAM'S JAW TIGHTENED as he studied Barry Inman.

He'd been hiding out for a reason. And Liam and his brother Jacob intended to find out why.

"I did not set that fire," Inman snapped. "I've told you that a dozen times." He ran a finger through the scraggly strands of his beard. "You have no right to hold me."

Liam folded his arms while Jacob leaned against the wall, a silent force of anger as he shot Inman a look of intimidation that would normally make a man wither.

"We have every right," Liam said. "You have been wanted for questioning in this arson case, which by the way has been upgraded to multiple homicides, for five years. But you disappeared to evade the law. That makes you look guilty as hell."

Panic zinged through the man's gray eyes. "I didn't murder anyone. I would never."

Liam slammed his hand on the table in front of Inman. "Then why did you run?"

He shifted in the metal chair. "Because you guys were trying to pin that fire and those deaths on me." Bitterness laced Inman's voice. "You didn't want to listen to the truth. You just wanted someone to blame, and I was the easy choice."

"Nothing about this case has been easy," Jacob interjected. "We lost our own father in that blaze."

"That's what I mean," Inman screeched. "You have a personal vendetta against me."

Liam forced a calm to his voice, although he was sorely tempted to beat the man into admitting what he'd done. "We just want the truth. And if you didn't set the fire, you may have information that could help us."

Inman looked down at his hands which were cuffed to the scarred metal table. "What makes you think that?"

Liam's patience was fading fast. "Because you ran, and you have motive."

"That doesn't mean I'm guilty."

"Then help us determine who is," Jacob said. "You filed that lawsuit and were angry when it was thrown out."

"Of course, I was mad. My wife died and it was the hospital's fault."

"Tell us what happened," Liam said. "Why you think they're to blame?"

Inman glanced back and forth between him and Jacob, his eyes narrowed. "It's not like you're going to believe me. No one did back then."

Summoning his self-control, Liam stood, calm, forceful, steel in his eyes. He'd waited five years. He could wait this bastard out until he convinced him to talk. "All right. If you don't want to cooperate, I'll escort you to your cell." He reached for the man's arm, but Inman jerked away.

"Wait, all right?" Inman barked.

Liam cocked one eye at him. "Are you going to tell us what happened?"

Inman gave a small nod. "My wife was having trouble catching her breath, said she was having chest pains. I thought she was having a heart attack, so I rushed her to the ER."

"Go on," Liam said.

Inman ran a hand over his face, his voice thickening with emotions. "They took her in right away, said they needed to do tests to figure out the cause. Then one of the nurses gave her some kind of medication, but that only made her worse and she stopped breathing." Tears filled the man's eyes. "Then she…just died."

Liam considered the man's story. "Why do you think the hospital was at fault?"

"Because I heard another nurse question the doctor," Inman said. "They were whispering, and she looked upset and told him something wasn't right."

Liam tensed and glanced at Jacob who frowned at the man's statement.

"You filed a lawsuit based on that?" Liam asked.

"Not at first. I tried to talk to the doctor about it. But he said I was off base and denied the conversation. Said I was just upset and misunderstood. But later, I saw that nurse talking to another man in scrubs. She looked all nervous-like and hurried away."

"She could have simply been upset over losing a patient," Jacob cut in.

Inman hesitated. "Look, I know what I heard and saw." He flexed his fingers on the table. "She knew something but clammed up. That's when I hired the lawyer. He talked to the doc and staff, but that damn nurse denied the conversation."

"Then what happened?" Liam coaxed.

Inman balled his hands into fists. "The lawyer subpoenaed records, but before he received them, the case was thrown out. I was so upset and insistent that he promised to move forward. He still intended to obtain those records, but then that fire broke out and the records were all destroyed." Inman glared up at Liam. "I wanted those records to prove I was right," Inman said bleakly. "So, if anything, that blows my motive to hell."

Liam and Jacob exchanged looks, then Liam set a notepad on the table. "Write down the nurse's name."

Surprise flickered in Inman's eyes. "You believe me?"

The verdict was still out. "I told you I want the truth. That means running my own investigation." Liam leaned over, palms on the table, and gave Inman a cold look.

"But if I find out you're lying or that you did set that fire, you're going to rot in prison for the rest of your life."

PEYTON TOSSED AND TURNED all night. Finally, a little after dawn, she gave up the attempt to sleep, rose, dressed in yoga pants and a T-shirt and went for a run.

As her feet pounded the pavement on the running trail around the lake where residents at Golden Gardens liked to gather, she fought guilt. She'd known Barry Inman had been a person of interest in the hospital fire because of his lawsuit. She'd understood his anger at the staff and the system and sympathized with him.

The police should have investigated his allegations more thoroughly. Except there had been no evidence.

She'd kept her suspicions to herself when the sheriff had questioned her about Gloria Inman's death. If she had spoken up, maybe the truth would have come out, and Barry wouldn't have harbored such rage.

The memory of almost losing her mother made her chest tighten. Her mother had sacrificed to help Peyton attend nursing school and supported her financially and emotionally while she'd studied for her boards.

Peyton had to protect her.

But guilt weighed on her. Had others died in that fire because of her silence?

Perspiration trickled down her neck and into her sports bra as she increased her pace and circled the lake. By the time she completed the run, the lawn was filling with residents enjoying breakfast on the patio.

She jogged back to the small apartment complex where she and some of the other staff members lived, let herself inside and hurried to shower before she had to report for duty. Praying the police discovered the truth about the fire and Inman's wife's death without involving her, she scrubbed her body and hair, then rinsed off, climbed from the shower and threw on her robe.

Just as she set the coffee to brew, her doorbell dinged. She automatically tensed. Who would be at her house this early in the morning? Maybe one of the other nurses?

She quickly dressed and finger combed her tangled

wet hair. Although a feeling of foreboding washed over her as she opened the door. A broad-shouldered dark-haired man stood on her stoop, towering over her. He stared at her with intimidating dark eyes.

"Peyton Weiss?"

Peyton swallowed hard. "Yes."

"Special Agent Liam Maverick." He flashed his credentials. "I need to ask you some questions about the death of Gloria Inman."

Peyton's stomach seized into a knot. Had her day of reckoning finally arrived?

Chapter Two

Liam had done his homework. RN Peyton Weiss was on duty the night Inman's wife had died.

It was all in his father's initial police report.

"I need you to come with me," Liam said.

Surprise and an emotion akin to fear flickered in her sky-blue eyes. "What is this about?"

"The hospital fire in Whistler five years ago. We made an arrest last night. A man named Barry Inman. You may remember him."

She didn't bother to lie. "Of course. But can't we just talk here?"

Liam squared his shoulders. Peyton Weiss was a gorgeous woman. She must have just stepped from the shower, because her hair was a damp, sexy mess.

He forced that thought at bay. This woman might hold the key to his father's death. He couldn't afford to see her as anything but a lead. Or a suspect.

Although he'd already spoken to her boss, Director Richard Jameson, and he painted the woman as an angel. Claimed she was the kindest, most caring, devoted, conscientious nurse to ever work for Golden Gardens.

But was that angel a disguise?

"I'd rather do it at the police station." The building itself would probably intimidate her. Maybe into talking.

She tensed, curled her fingers around the edge of the door, then glanced at the clock on the opposite wall. "I have to go to work soon. My patients depend on me for medications."

She was stalling. "This is important. Tell them you're going to be late."

Her lips pressed into a thin line at his order, but he didn't back down. If she refused, he'd haul her into the station in handcuffs.

"My *patients* are important," she said curtly. "Let me call and arrange for one of the other nurses to cover for me."

He stepped inside the entryway while she went to retrieve her phone. He glanced around the living room and kitchen. Simple, comfortable furnishings, a color scheme of gray and blue, a book on the table, water glass. Everything appeared neat and orderly.

"Yes, Joanna," he heard her say. "I'm not sure how long I'll be gone. Can you cover for me, and check on Mama?"

A pause. "Okay, thanks. I'll text you as soon as I get back."

He chewed the inside of his cheek. *If* she came back. If he sensed she was lying or withholding information, he might throw her in a holding cell for the night just like he had Barry Inman.

She returned a minute later with her keys, then jammed her phone in her purse.

He gestured toward the keys. "You won't need those. I'm driving."

She frowned. "But I'll need my car to get back."

"I'll bring you home after we finish."

Alarm seeped into her eyes, but she clamped her lips tight and stepped out the door. He waited while she locked it, then led her to his black SUV. Her gaze skated over the interior of his vehicle as she slid into the passenger seat, and she strapped on her seat belt with shaky hands.

He pressed the accelerator, ignoring the tiny twinge of guilt he had for intimidating her. Heaven help him. She did look like an angel, and had the voice of one, too.

But he'd learned the hard way not to allow himself to get distracted by a pretty woman.

PEYTON SAT IN SILENCE as the federal agent drove toward Whistler. His last name was Maverick. The sheriff who'd questioned her regarding the circumstances surrounding Inman's wife's death had been a Maverick, one who'd died in the fire.

His four sons had been devastated. She'd seen their pictures on the news. Seen the pain and anguish. Her heart had ached for them just as it had for Barry.

The oldest son, Jacob, stepped in as sheriff. He'd been a formidable force when he'd interviewed her about the fire.

Barry Inman was their prime suspect. Did the police have new evidence against him?

She twisted her hands together, struggling to remain calm as the mountains and countryside rolled past. The rich golds, reds and oranges on the trees were starting to fade and the ground was littered with brittle, dead leaves.

Golden Gardens was situated in a small community called River's Edge about twenty minutes from Whistler. The quaint little town catered to tourists, kayakers, and featured a special Christmas village and festival each year that drew people from across the country.

With each mile Special Agent Maverick put between her and Golden Gardens though, her anxiety mounted. Just because the FBI wanted to talk to her didn't mean they knew anything.

But worry for her mother intensified. She'd given Jo strict instructions that no one was to administer any medication to her except Joanna, and that she was not allowed any strange visitors. Joanna had been curious about her precautions, but Peyton emphasized that her mother had anxiety attacks when encountering unfamiliar people.

Not that having strange visitors was common. No one came to see her mother except her.

As they neared Whistler, the haunting memory of that fire hammered at her conscience. Was Inman's wife's death related to the fire? Was the fire related to the mistake in the ER?

Had her silence allowed an arsonist and killer to go free?

The agent slowed as they passed the new hospital and images of the terrified patients and staff flooded her. She heard their screams at night when she closed her eyes. Sometimes she saw the families hovering over injured ones. And then there were the graves of the people, both patients and staff, who hadn't survived. The town council had erected a memorial at the new facility to honor the victims.

They passed a small shopping strip where remnants of a building that had recently been destroyed by fire remained. Joy's Nail Salon. She'd seen that story on the news a few months ago.

The other storefronts looked like they'd been given a fresh coat of paint. The town square where she'd once enjoyed picnics with her mother looked empty, probably due to the impending storm. A little café called Mitzi's had opened up, and The Brew, the coffee shop on the corner, still remained, along with the bookstore.

Agent Maverick parked in front of the sheriff's office, then came around and opened the door for her. She felt eyes of locals watching her from across the street and was grateful he hadn't handcuffed her and brought her in, siren blaring.

As he led her inside and she faced the sheriff, the past met the present. Sheriff Maverick looked just as tough and intimidating as he had five years ago. Standing side by side, the brothers presented one solid wall of steely resolve and scrutinizing eyes that sent a shiver down her spine.

"Ms. Weiss," Sheriff Maverick said in clipped acknowledgment.

She murmured hello, but the word barely came out for the emotions clogging her throat.

The sheriff gestured toward a set of double doors. "Let's go back here to talk."

Special Agent Maverick gripped her arm and gestured for her to follow his brother. Peyton had the eerie sense that she was walking toward a cell, not a room for a friendly chat. Nerves on edge, she mentally reviewed the statement she'd given the sheriff during her first interview regarding Inman. She had to stick with her story.

Only then would her mother be safe.

LIAM ESCORTED PEYTON into the interrogation room, battling instincts that she was innocent. She'd certainly seemed worried about her mother when he'd overheard her conversation with her coworker, Joanna.

He needed to speak to that woman in private. She might know if Peyton was keeping something from the police. The fact that Peyton had moved her mother from Whistler shortly after the fire would raise suspicion, except that the hospital had literally been shut down for months during the initial investigation and rebuilding.

Staff had been relocated, transferred, quit. People had been traumatized, dealing with personal injuries and losses and PTSD. Mixed reactions from the town confused the situation. Some wanted to nail the person who'd set the fire, others were too in shock to recall details of what happened that night, and some wanted to move on and forget the tragic event entirely.

Which category did Peyton fall into?

Liam studied Peyton's body language as she sank into the chair, looking for signs of guilt or panic as if she was on the run.

So far, she had no motive herself for setting the fire. Unless she'd set it on principle to prove the hospital was at fault for Inman's wife's death. But doing so would have put others at risk, and she would have known that.

She didn't fit the profile of that type of perpetrator.

She fidgeted, then knotted her hands in her lap and pressed her lips into a thin line.

Liam claimed the chair opposite her, the tension in the room palpable.

"Now, why did you drag me from my apartment and my patients?" Peyton asked, her tone slightly irritated.

Liam raised a brow, surprised by her direct approach. "I told you that we arrested Barry Inman last night."

She gave a little nod. "I saw it on the news. You think he set that deadly fire because his wife's lawsuit was thrown out?"

At least she wasn't playing dumb. Then again, maybe she wasn't surprised to see him at her door.

Because she was hiding something and had expected at some point for the buck to land back at her feet?

Jacob took the seat beside Liam. "Do you remember talking to my father, Sheriff Maverick, five years ago regarding the death of Inman's wife?"

Her throat muscles worked as she swallowed. "Of course." She leaned forward, her expression intense. "I told him everything I knew about the woman's unfortunate death. Which was nothing."

"Tell us again," Liam said. "Just to refresh our memories."

She inhaled a deep breath. "I was in the ER when Gloria Inman was brought in. She was unconscious, struggling to breathe and in cardiac distress. The doctor ordered medication, performed CPR, then brought in the crash cart." She squeezed her eyes closed for a moment as if reliving a troubling memory. "I'm sorry to say she…didn't make it. We tried everything, but sometimes it's just impossible."

"I have the statement you gave Inman's attorney," Liam said. "According to Inman, he overheard you tell another nurse that something went wrong. Is that true?"

She crossed her legs beneath the table. "Mr. Inman was understandably upset, distraught and in shock," she said, then pressed a hand over her heart. "Often times families of patients lash out when a loved one is ill or in pain, especially if they don't survive. They think the doctors and nurses are gods and can save everyone." Her voice warbled. "But we're not. We're only human, and sometimes no matter what you do, you lose a patient."

Liam's throat felt thick. He sure as hell understood that. He and his brothers had tried to save their father and failed.

Jacob cleared his throat. "Ms. Weiss, Barry Inman threatened revenge against the hospital for the alleged negligence. Did he ever personally threaten you?"

His question seemed to suck the air from Peyton's lungs. She rubbed her fingers together in a nervous gesture, then dropped them in her lap. "No. He didn't personally threaten me."

Liam arched a brow. The question upset her because she was hiding something. "But you heard him threaten others at the hospital?"

"That's not what I meant."

Liam stared her directly in the eye. "Then what did you mean?"

"Just what I said. That he didn't threaten me." She sat back and tapped her foot. "Look, I've cooperated and told you everything I know. I'm truly sorry for Mrs. Inman's death, but I don't have any more information regarding it than I did five years ago."

Her answer sounded practiced. Defensive. Which raised more questions in Liam's mind. "Ms. Weiss, do you think Barry Inman started the fire at the Whistler Hospital?"

"I really don't know." She pushed away from the table. "Now if that's all, I need to get back to my patients and my mother."

Liam gritted his teeth. "Sit down, Ms. Weiss," he

said firmly. "You aren't going anywhere until you tell us everything you remember about the night of the fire."

ALARM BELLS RANG in Peyton's mind. Did the agent believe she'd seen the person who'd set the fire?

Both men glared at her and she sank onto the cold metal chair. She directed her comment to the sheriff. "I don't have anything to add from my previous statement."

Sheriff Maverick shifted. "Indulge us. We need to hear your personal account again."

She lifted her chin. "Are you questioning everyone else who was there that night?"

The men exchanged furtive looks. "We will if we need to," the sheriff replied.

"In light of the fact that we found Mr. Inman, we're reviewing all the statements from witnesses, patients, staff and bystanders," the agent said. "Sometimes after the passage of time, people recall details they didn't notice or remember immediately following an incident. We're hoping that's the case with you."

Peyton stifled a reaction. His logic made perfect sense.

"So, tell us exactly what happened that night," Agent Maverick said. "Starting with the time you reported for work."

Peyton massaged her temple where a headache was starting to pulse. "I had a twelve-hour shift in the ER, 7:00 a.m. to 7:00 p.m. The day was fairly calm, routine patients. Flu, a broken arm, one man presented with stroke symptoms. Just a normal day."

And her mother was in the hospital being treated for

pneumonia. She was receiving IV antibiotics, fluids and breathing treatments.

"Did you see anything out of the ordinary during your shift?" the agent asked. "A disgruntled family member of a patient? Maybe someone wanting drugs that roused your suspicion?"

Peyton wrinkled her brow. "Actually, there was a young man who appeared to be homeless. He was on the list we keep of repeat drug seekers, so we turned him away."

"A list?" the agent asked.

She nodded. "All hospitals, especially ERs, keep a list of people who repeatedly come in with fake illnesses in an attempt to get prescriptions."

"Did this guy become belligerent or aggressive?" the sheriff asked.

"Not that I recall," Peyton said. "Security escorted him out the ER exit. That was it."

The agent leaned forward. "Do you remember his name?"

"No, I'm afraid not. It would have been in the records though."

"You mean the ones that burned in that fire?" Sheriff Maverick replied.

Peyton shifted. "Yes."

"How about Barry Inman?" Special Agent Maverick asked. "Did you see him at the hospital that night?"

Peyton massaged her temple again. "I really don't recall. Once the fire broke out, it was chaos. People were running and screaming and panicked. Everyone pitched in to help evacuate the building. Firefighters were everywhere—the flames were spreading."

The agent gave her a pointed stare. "How about on the lawn?"

She closed her eyes and envisioned the scene. She'd been in action mode helping patients outside. Had been desperate to find her mother.

Had Inman been there?

Chapter Three

Peyton gave a small shrug. "I don't remember seeing Mr. Inman in the hospital or outside that night. But it was so hectic. Everyone was scared. Families looking for loved ones, patients needing help, first responders dashing onto the scene to assist and directing people to get out." She sighed. "My mother was also in the hospital with pneumonia, so after I helped clear the ER, I was frantic to find her."

"But you did?" the agent asked.

Peyton's breath quickened. "One of the doctors was performing CPR when I reached her." Dr. Butler, the same doctor she'd reported her suspicions to. "He saved her life."

The other nurses adored him, too. Thought he was a saint in the ER. He'd mentored her, also.

She'd begun to wonder if she'd misread the situation with Inman's wife, and Dr. Butler was simply trying to protect her from criminal charges by encouraging her silence.

Special Agent Maverick leaned across the table again. "Are you all right, Ms. Weiss?"

She exhaled and pulled herself from the memory. "Yes, it was just a scary night." Her gaze met his. "I understand that your father died saving others. I'm sorry for your loss."

The agent's jaw tightened, and the sheriff released a wary breath. A tense heartbeat passed.

"He did lose his life that night, along with many others," the agent finally said. "And we are going to get to the bottom of what happened. If there's anything else you can tell us that might help, we need you to speak up."

Peyton's heart squeezed. She wanted to tell him everything. But she wasn't sure of anything anymore.

"I wish I *could* tell you who set that fire, but I honestly don't know. One of my coworkers, a PA, was seriously injured and still has scars." Eileen's battered body taunted her. "She suffered second-degree burns and a falling beam crushed her leg. She underwent physical therapy for months to learn to walk again. She can't lift patients or do her job now and suffers from PTSD." Peyton shuddered. She suspected Eileen was addicted to pain pills, too, and had encouraged her husband to seek help.

"I'm sorry about your friend," the agent said. "Where is she now?"

"She and her husband moved to Asheville. He said they needed a change of scenery." She understood that. Just driving back through Whistler resurrected her own tumultuous memories.

The sheriff dropped a file onto the desk. "I reviewed my father's notes on the initial investigation into Inman's claims. According to Inman's statement, you were talking to another nurse and implied something was wrong."

Peyton ground her molars to control her temper. This

was not a chat. It was an interrogation. They kept asking the same questions over and over hoping to catch her in a lie.

The sheriff tapped the file. "But you denied making any statement indicating wrongdoing on the part of the staff." He hesitated, the air tense with his scrutiny.

"That's correct."

The agent leaned back in his chair. "Why would he say that if it wasn't true?"

"As I said before, he was distraught and in shock and desperate to blame someone."

A skeptical look marred Sheriff Maverick's face. "Then you stand by your original statement, that you don't believe the hospital was responsible?"

She had her doubts. Ones she couldn't share. "I do." She heaved another breath, her body teeming with anxiety. "Now, can I go? I need to check on my mother. She gets disoriented if I don't show up at certain times."

The brothers traded looks again, then Liam stood and adjusted his holster. "Yes, for now. I'll drive you back."

She wanted to be anywhere but in the car with the intimidating, handsome federal agent. He made her want to talk, to help him. To make sure justice was served for all the people hurt five years ago.

But confiding in him was impossible, so she forced herself to remain calm, not confrontational.

She could fall apart later when she was alone.

LIAM AND JACOB left Peyton in the room alone to stew for a moment while they conferred outside the door.

"What do you think?" Liam asked Jacob.

Jacob muttered a sound of frustration. "I don't know. Dad made a notation that he suspected she was holding back something. When I questioned her after the fire, she was a wreck. Seemed nervous and jumpy. But then again, everyone who worked at the hospital was upset and a wreck, too."

"So were the family members who'd lost loved ones," Liam added. "People were emotional and in shock and trying to pick up the pieces of their lives. She did say her mother almost died that night, too."

"True. The staff was also defensive. Dodging blame. Some of the families wanted to point fingers at the hospital. Others at individuals who they thought had enemies," Jacob added. "And then we became sidetracked thinking the fire was set as a diversion for the kidnapping of Cora's baby."

"That was a logical assumption," Liam agreed, remembering the press descending. Their focus had been on the terrified mother who'd just delivered a little girl only to have her ripped away in the midst of the chaos.

Because he was the oldest, Jacob thought he had to take care of him and his brothers, and their mother, and stepped into his father's shoes as sheriff.

The case of the missing baby had taken priority over Jacob's own grief at the time. When the case had gone cold, he'd blamed himself.

"Stop beating yourself up over the past, Jacob. You found Cora's little girl and her kidnapper is in prison where she belongs," Liam said.

Jacob smiled. "But Cora suffered terribly until we did."

"She's happy now and she loves you, bro." Liam patted his brother's arm. "And now your family is growing."

A real smile lit Jacob's eyes. "I am a lucky man. Another month and my son will be here." He gave Liam an odd look. "I hope you find someone someday, too. You deserve it, Liam."

Did he? His last conversation with his father echoed in his head. His father suggested he take a deputy's position in Whistler just as Jacob had. But Liam had argued, insisted he wanted more than to be a small-town deputy. He wanted to make a difference, work big cases, real investigations.

His father had looked hurt but said he understood. Liam had kicked himself every day since that conversation. He'd made his father feel his work wasn't big enough, good enough. But his father had put his life on the line to protect the citizens in Whistler and the mountains they called home. He'd also been a good father and a devoted husband.

What could be more important than that?

Liam would give anything to turn back time. To take back the hurtful words. To tell his father how much he loved and admired him. That everything he'd aspired to do was because he wanted to make his father proud.

"Liam?" Jacob murmured. "You okay?"

Liam blinked to banish the painful images from his mind. "Yeah. Maybe once this case is solved and we get justice for Dad, I can think about it." But not until then. He'd waited too long to see his father's killer pay to let anything interfere.

"About the origin of the fire," he said, steering his mind back on track. "Griff and the evidence-response team agreed that the point of origin was near the ER, in one of the storage rooms that held chemical supplies. Which was beside the records room."

"That's right."

A scenario took shape in Liam's mind. "If Inman

was right about negligence in his wife's death and there was a record of it in her file, perhaps the fire was set to destroy that evidence."

Jacob made a clucking sound with his tongue. "If Peyton made the mistake and her job was on the line, and she was sole provider for her mother who was ill, maybe she was desperate and set the fire to destroy proof of wrongdoing. Then the fire got out of control."

Liam tried to reconcile the compassionate nurse her coworkers bragged about with a woman who'd take a risk by doing such a thing. But he couldn't quite make the scenario fit.

"I considered that. But the director at Golden Gardens sang Peyton's praises. It's hard to believe she'd endanger lives like that."

Jacob worked his mouth from side to side. "She seemed awfully antsy when we questioned her."

His brother had noticed it, too. Peyton presented a calm front. But the little twinge at the corners of her eyes and the way she didn't quite make eye contact was a tell.

She was holding something back.

"Look into her financials while I drive her back to her apartment," Liam said. "Maybe she didn't set the fire, but she knows something and was paid to keep quiet."

Jacob nodded agreement. "I'll see if I can track down the other staff members on duty in the ER the night of Inman's wife's death. They didn't divulge anything to Dad, but if they learn we suspect that case is connected to the fire, someone might decide to talk."

True. Covering for an accidental mistake with a patient was one thing. But covering for an arsonist who caused multiple deaths might be heinous enough to convince a witness to come forward.

EARLY AFTERNOON SHADOWS fell across the winding mountain road as Special Agent Maverick drove Peyton back toward Golden Gardens.

With days growing shorter and clouds moving in, the misty fog rolling off the ridges and steep cliffs painted the world a smoky, eerie gray, a reminder leaves were dying, and winter would soon barrel around the corner.

Peyton shifted, knotting her hands in her lap. The FBI agent's gaze was scrutinizing her every movement. She couldn't blink without the sense that he was analyzing her and finding her lacking.

She'd never met a more intimidating man.

Or a more ruggedly handsome one. Instead of a suit and badge, he looked like he should be wearing a cowboy hat, tight jeans and boots and riding across the wilderness atop a stallion with the sun slanting off his chiseled face.

Heaven help her. The fact that she'd noticed his good looks was pathetic. Had to be due to the fact that she hadn't dated in over five years. She'd been afraid to get close to anyone.

Afraid they'd see that she was a liar.

She swallowed hard. She had to maintain her composure for a few more minutes. Then she'd be back in her own place and she could crash in upon herself.

He cleared his throat. "How is your mother's health?"

The question took her off guard and seemed innocuous enough. Except she had a feeling that everything this man did was calculating and meant to extract information he could use against her.

"She's seventy-nine so dealing with multiple health issues," she replied. "RA, a thyroid condition and her memory's starting to slip."

"That's the reason you moved her to Golden Gardens? She needs assisted living?"

Again, she felt as if he was using his interrogation skills on her. "Yes." She had to keep her answers as honest as possible. Still, she refrained from explaining that the security measures had also been a draw.

"Why did you take a job there instead of another hospital?"

His voice sounded concerned, not accusatory. Was he trying to wear her down by winning her trust? "I enjoy working with elderly patients," she answered. "There's a huge need for good medical and memory care for seniors. I also wanted to be close to my mother for as long as she's around."

"Do you have siblings who help out or visit?"

Peyton shook her head. She did have a younger sister. The pain from watching the addiction take control of her life until she was living on the streets wrenched at her heart. The realization that Val had sold her body for a fix caused her mother to have a nervous breakdown at one point. Peyton had worked hard to help her mother recover. But Val's disappearance from their lives hurt as much as if they'd buried her. Maybe more, because each day they lived with the worry of where she might be, if she was hurt or sick. If she might turn up dead in a ditch or an alley.

But she didn't like to talk about her sister.

"No, no family, just me. I promised Mama I'd be there for her, and I intend to keep that promise."

"That's admirable."

She cut her eyes toward him, almost believing him. But he was an expert at his job and although he hadn't arrested her, the Miranda Warning she'd seen on TV crime shows echoed in her head. *Anything you say can and will be used against you in a court of law...*

She jerked her gaze back to the road. She didn't want to go to prison. Or for him to see that pain in her eyes. Pain she'd learned to live with. Pain she didn't intend on sharing.

They lapsed into a strained silence as he veered past the turn to the heart of River's Edge and followed the road leading to Golden Gardens. Nestled in the mountains, away from town, the facility offered privacy and serenity to its residents and patients. Its location and security gate also helped waylay passersby from venturing onto the property.

Her trust in strangers had been shattered five years ago. Not knowing who'd threatened her made her suspicious of every man she met.

Special Agent Maverick stopped at the gate, identified himself and was buzzed through. He followed the narrow road leading to her apartment complex in silence. The white brick building was flanked by giant live oaks and pines with the mountains rising behind.

Ever cautious, she scanned the property and was relieved to see her car still in its place. The fog thickened, enveloping her building in that same smoky gray that gave her a chill.

The agent parked, climbed out and came around to her door, but she'd already stepped from the SUV, anxious to escape his scrutiny.

His dark eyes narrowed as if he'd read her mind. "I'll walk you to your door."

"That's not necessary," Peyton said. "I have to relieve the nurse who took over my patients today and check on Mama. She'll be wondering where I am."

He stood ramrod straight, his look so intense that a shudder coursed up her spine. Then he removed a card from his pocket and offered it to her. "Ms. Weiss, please call me if you remember anything else about the night Inman's wife died, or about the night of the fire." His gaze settled over her, rattling her even more. "I know you want justice in both matters just as I do."

Guilt nearly choked her, but she simply nodded and took the card. His fingers felt warm as they brushed hers, a sharp contrast to the coldness in his eyes. She wondered if he ever smiled.

It didn't matter, she told herself as she unlocked her door and hurried to change into her scrubs. He was FBI.

As soon as she was dressed, she texted Joanna that she was back. She spent the next three hours tending to her assigned patients and doling out medications, then helping them to PT and to dinner. Her mother looked agitated when she joined her at their usual table.

"This strange man was here today," her mother said as she wiped her mouth with a napkin.

Agent Maverick hadn't spoken to her mother. He'd come straight to her place. "A man? Who was it?"

"I don't know." Her voice cracked the way it did sometimes when she struggled with her words. "But I didn't like him. He smelled like cigarettes and sweat."

Maybe her mother was just confused. Sometimes her memories blurred, and the past mingled with the present. Peyton's father had been a smoker and died of lung cancer when she was just a kid.

"Did you talk to this man?" Peyton asked.

Her mother sniffed and pushed away her plate, her vegetables uneaten. "No, but he said he left something for you."

Peyton went stone still. "For me? What was it?"

Her mother toyed with her napkin, folding it one way then another, as she did when she was agitated. "I don't know, dear, but I was glad when he left," she muttered. "I told Fred, and he checked around outside, but he said no one was there. Said my eyes were playing tricks on me." A hint of fear that the security guard was right made her mother's voice quiver.

But fear slithered through Peyton. On another day, she might dismiss her mother's comment as paranoia related to her dementia. But in light of the news report, Inman's arrest and the fact that the FBI had shown up at her door, she couldn't ignore it.

Chapter Four

Liam's phone buzzed just as he reached the sheriff's office in Whistler. Early evening shadows cast a grayness over the town, made drearier by the storm clouds above. Already the days were growing shorter, night setting in and drowning the area in darkness long before Liam was ready to call it a day.

He punched Connect.

"It's Bennett," his partner at the Bureau said. "I've been looking into Peyton Weiss's financials, but haven't found anything suspicious. The woman seems squeaky clean. Not even a parking ticket. And no complaints ever filed regarding her work."

"Except for her name being mentioned by Barry Inman," Liam said.

"Yeah, that's true. But you got me thinking, so I obtained a list of every staff member who worked at Whistler Hospital around the time of the fire, and also ones who left within six months prior to the fire."

"Did you find anything?"

"That's a serious list," Bennett said with a chuckle. "It's going to take some time to go through them."

It had already been five damn years. But Bennett was new to the case and they could use a set of fresh eyes.

Bennett cut straight to business as usual. "So far, I did find one name you should check out. A med tech, Herbert Brantley. Thirty-five, works at River's Edge Hospital now. But a few months after the Whistler fire, he made some fairly big purchases. A cabin on the lake, an expensive convertible and custom motorcycle."

"The man likes to play," Liam said. "But where did he get that kind of money?"

"That's what I'm trying to figure out," Bennett said. "I'll let you know when I get some answers."

"Any reports of misconduct or problems on the job?" Liam asked.

"Not that I've found. But I'll dig deeper."

"Jacob and I will go have a talk with him. Text me his address."

"It's coming your way."

"I have another job for you, too," Liam said. "Peyton Weiss mentioned the hospital kept a list of drug seekers who strike the ERs. She said security escorted a homeless man from the hospital that night. Hospital records were destroyed in the fire, but if he was a repeat offender, he might have gone to an urgent care or another hospital close by."

"On it," Bennett agreed.

Liam ended the call, then climbed from his vehicle and walked up to Jacob's office. Jacob met him at the door. "Did Peyton Weiss reveal anything more on the way home?"

Liam shook his head. "We just talked about her ailing mother. She's pretty devoted to her."

"She's hiding something," Jacob said. "I can feel it in my bones."

Liam gritted his teeth. "Me, too. Anything else from Inman?"

"He insists Peyton is lying, that he knows what he heard."

"My partner may have a lead. We need to have a chat with a med tech named Herbert Brantley."

Jacob's brows rose. "Who's he?"

"A former employee at the hospital who came into a boatload of money after the fire."

PEYTON SEARCHED HER MOTHER'S cottage for something the mystery man had left inside but found nothing. Had her mother imagined the incident?

Breathing a sigh of relief, she waited for her mother to get ready for bed, grateful she could still feed and dress herself. It was so sad when the residents got past that stage. Losing their dignity was the hardest cross to bear.

A smile glowed on her mother's pale cheeks as Peyton tucked her in and made sure she had water beside her bed. Her mother brushed Peyton's cheek with her frail hand. "I treasure every day with you, honey."

Tears burned the backs of Peyton's eyelids, but she blinked them away. "I'm glad we're together, Mama." The very reason she had to keep her silence about the past.

She claimed the rocking chair by her mother's bed, then read their daily devotional and they said a prayer before her mother fell asleep.

Peyton enjoyed their nightly rituals almost as much as her mother seemed to. Sometimes she read poems from her mother's favorite poetry book, inspirational quotes or devotionals. Other times, they reflected on the day and past memories. They ended each night and morning with a simple prayer.

Her mother enjoyed sharing stories about when Peyton was little, and Peyton was starved for memories about how her mother had grown up on a working cotton farm. Although her grandparents had died when she was small, Peyton had gotten to know them through her mother's nostalgic tales.

The days were growing shorter outside with fall, and so was her mother's memory. Doctors called it sundowner's syndrome, where elderly people became confused at night because of the lack of light. Some grew agitated and depressed. They lost track of time. Depression and disorientation were serious side effects.

All the more reason she made it a point to encourage the seniors to sit outside and enjoy the sunlight during the day. She needed the fresh air and sunshine herself.

Her mother's comment about the stranger still disturbed her. Dr. Sweetwater, the geriatrician on staff, warned her that dementia could cause hallucinations, especially in the wake of UT infections, a recurring problem with her mother and worse with the patients in the nursing home who were bedridden.

She pressed a kiss on her mother's cheek, then covered her with the candlewicked quilt she'd helped her mother make ten years ago before her mother's hands grew too gnarled and twisted with arthritis to sew. Worry needled her, and she stood and watched her sleep for a few minutes before leaving the room. "I promise I'll always take care of you, Mama."

Satisfied she was resting, she checked the lock on the window in the bedroom, then went into the den and tidied up.

Before she left for her own apartment, she checked all the window locks along with the French doors.

Weary and exhausted from the strain of the day, she walked out to her car, but scanned the parking lot and property for anyone lurking around. Something moved in the trees behind the building. Near the rose garden.

Peyton went still, her heart stuttering. Had her mother been right about a stranger being at Golden Gardens today?

HERBERT BRANTLEY LIVED in the small town of River's Edge, about thirty miles from Whistler and not far from Golden Gardens.

"How's Cora doing?" Liam asked as Jacob drove around the mountain.

"She's ready to have this baby and see her toes again," Jacob said with a chuckle.

Liam grinned. Ever since Jacob got married, he'd softened, become a family man. But that was okay. His brother deserved to be happy.

Jacob veered down the winding road for a mile, then turned onto a graveled drive. His SUV bounced over the ruts as he drove, tires grinding gravel. A half mile later, a rustic A-framed cabin slipped into view. Liam spotted the Harley parked beneath a carport beside what he assumed was the convertible which was draped in a car cover.

Jacob parked, and they surveyed the property as they walked up to the door together. Jacob knocked, and they waited several seconds before the door opened. A short, stocky guy in sweats stood in the doorway with a beer in his hand. His hair was scruffy, a scar ran along his right eyebrow and his nose looked as if it had been broken more than once.

"Herbert Brantley?" Jacob asked.

Herbert's gaze shot back and forth between them, then his eyes narrowed, and he rocked back on his feet. "Yeah. What's going on?"

Jacob introduced both of them and Liam flashed his credentials. "We'd like to talk to you about the Whistler Hospital fire. May we come in?"

"Now?" The man hesitated and glanced over his shoulder. Did he have company?

"Yes, now. It won't take but a few minutes," Jacob said. "And it's important."

The man raked his fingers through his hair, then sighed. "All right. Just wait here a minute." He closed the door, leaving them on the stoop.

"He's hiding something." Jacob laid his hand over his weapon. "Maybe drugs?"

"Could be." Liam jiggled the doorknob and opened the door. He stepped inside, braced for trouble, and saw Herbert coming from the bathroom. The sound of the toilet flushing echoed from the hall. "Guess he just got rid of it."

Jacob cursed, then Herbert spotted them and halted in the hallway. "I thought you were waiting outside."

"We got cold," Liam said, daring the guy to argue. He gestured toward the living area. "Now, sit down, Herbert."

Herbert looked rattled but sank onto a brown leather sofa that looked worn. Two plaid chairs flanked the stone fireplace and a rustic coffee table sat in the center of the seating area. Apparently, he'd spent all his money on vehicles, not furniture.

"I don't understand why you're here now." Herbert scratched his belly. "That fire happened over five years ago."

"But the case was never solved. We're hoping you can add some insight."

Herbert rubbed the condensation on his beer can away with his beefy thumb. "I don't know how. I told the cops I didn't see anything suspicious."

"Where were you when the fire started?" Jacob asked.

"Working in the ER," he said. "The minute the alarm sounded, everyone flew into motion to help patients outside."

"You were in the ER with Nurse Weiss?" Liam asked.

Herbert glanced down at his fingers where he'd started tapping the armchair. "Yeah, although I was in another exam room with a potential stroke victim and Nurse Weiss was working on another case."

"Was she in the ER the entire time until the fire started, or did she leave at some point?" Jacob asked.

"Her patient was coding so she stepped out to get the crash cart."

Liam crossed his arms. "Was the cart stored anywhere near the records room?"

Herbert squinted as if confused. "The equipment is kept in the ER in its own room but readily available to whoever needs it. Necessary medication for emergencies is stored inside. It's locked and only the nurse has the code to open it."

"And that would have been Peyton?"

He nodded. "Yeah, she was the charge nurse."

"Did you see anyone suspicious in the ER or perhaps lurking in the hallway or the ER entrance?"

"Don't remember anything," Herbert said. "But like I told you, it was a busy night, and once the fire alarm sounded, it was total chaos. Firemen stormed the building, and the staff and visitors were rushing around trying to evacuate everyone."

It was the same story they'd heard from Peyton.

"I thought you had a suspect in the fire," Herbert said. "That guy whose wife died. He wanted revenge against the hospital or something."

"He is a person of interest," Jacob answered. "As a matter of fact, we have him in custody at the moment and have been questioning him."

Herbert's eyes widened in confusion, then worry. "He did it, didn't he?"

"We're not certain," Liam said. "You were on duty that night as well, weren't you?"

Liam studied Herbert's reaction. He looked as if he might run but fidgeted and then said yes. "But I wasn't in the ER. Peyton was."

Back to Peyton.

"Mr. Inman claims he overheard Nurse Weiss talking to someone about a mistake, but he's not specific. Do you know anything about that?"

Herbert gulped. "No. I heard he said that, but I have no idea what he was talking about."

He shrugged. "For the record, I liked Nurse Weiss. If she messed up, I'm sure it was an accident."

"Do *you* think she messed up?" Liam asked.

"That's not what I meant. I meant she's a good nurse and all."

Liam decided on another angle. "A few weeks after

the fire, you seemed to have come into some money." He gestured around the room. "You bought this house, and a car and motorcycle. Those items aren't cheap."

Herbert's posture went rigid. "What does that have to do with the fire?"

Jacob cleared his throat. "Where did you get the money, Herbert?"

Herbert stood. "That's none of your business."

Liam pinned him with an intimidating look. "It is, if someone paid you to keep quiet about Inman's wife's death. Or about who set that fire."

Herbert swung his hand toward the door. "You can leave now. I'm done talking."

The fact that he clammed up and grew so defensive roused Liam's suspicions. Had someone paid Herbert to keep him from talking?

Chapter Five

Peyton held her breath as she inched around the side of her mother's cottage and peered into the darkness. Yes, there was a shadow back there.

Someone was in the garden.

Fred, the security guard? But at this time of night?

She held her breath as she hovered by the corner of the building, watching. The shadow moved deeper into the garden and was hunched over, as if he was trying not to be seen.

Paranoid that her mother had been right about a stranger on the premises, she inched toward the garden, careful to stay at the edge of the tree line so she was shielded from sight. The gardener and residents who'd joined the gardening club had covered some of the plants in case of frost, and some of the plants had been trimmed in preparation for the winter.

A sound broke into the night, echoing from the concrete bench near the climbing roses, and she gripped her phone to call 9-1-1. But as she rounded the curved section of lilies before she reached the roses, a low humming echoed toward her. The song, "Amazing Grace." The shadow wasn't a prowler, but one of the patients, Leon Brittles, who was suffering from Alzheimer's.

Her heart broke as she watched him kneel in front of the angel statue. It wasn't the first time he'd come out there. At night, he often forgot where he was. He confused the rose garden with the memorial garden where he'd buried his wife, Hazel.

Quietly, she put her phone away, let him finish his ritual, then approached him. "Leon," she said softly. "What a beautiful night to visit your wife." She put her arm around him. "But it's getting chilly and it's time to go in."

He looked up at her dazed and confused, then a smile softened his eyes. "She likes it when I sing to her."

"I know she does," Peyton said gently. "But she wants you to be tucked in tonight while it's cold."

"There was the prettiest young girl here before you came," Leon said. "But she looked so sad. I heard her crying in the garden. That's why I came out."

Peyton inhaled a deep breath. Like her mother, Leon got confused. But he'd never talked about a young girl before. Maybe he was hallucinating about his wife when she was younger.

"Tell me about this girl," Peyton coaxed.

His eyes lit as he bobbed his head up and down. "She had long wavy black hair and was so pretty, but she looked so alone. When I spoke to her, she ran off. I reckon I scared her."

"Oh, Leon, you couldn't scare anyone away. I'm sure she was just tired and ready to call it a night." She rubbed his shoulder. "Come on, let's go inside." He stumbled slightly and she steadied him, then led him back to his cottage. By the time they reached his place, he was wobbling, and his eyes were closing. She settled him into his room, then locked the door and texted Fred.

He agreed to walk by Leon's cottage during the night and make sure he didn't wander outside again.

Then she drove back to her apartment. As she parked, she scanned the front of her building and the property, and saw another nurse heading into her own unit. Relieved that she recognized the cars in the parking lot as belonging to various staff members, she locked her car, then hurried up the sidewalk to her first-floor apartment. She'd chosen the bottom floor because she liked to step outside on her patio in the morning and enjoy her coffee and the view.

Foolish. It would have been wiser to have chosen the second floor where breaking in would be more difficult.

A gust of wind picked up, hurling dead leaves across the path and the trees swayed, branches bobbing up and down as if a storm was brewing. The scent of impending rain filled the air and thunder rumbled above.

She unlocked the door, wishing she had a security system, although when she'd approached management about one for the staff apartments, they'd claimed security systems were costly and unnecessary. The property was already secure. It was gated, and you needed a code to get onto the property.

Yet the woods behind the building offered numerous places to hide. Someone could park and sneak in through the woods, if they wanted to slip past security. She darted inside, flipped on the light and scanned the open living room/kitchen area. Everything appeared as she'd left it this morning when Agent Maverick had knocked on her door and carted her to the sheriff's office.

She locked her door, dropped her keys on the table

by it and headed to the kitchen for a drink of water. But a plain brown manila envelope caught her eye.

She went still, then glanced across the room again. Nothing was out of place.

But someone had been inside her apartment.

Fear sliced through her, and she grabbed a kitchen knife and slowly inched through her apartment to the hall. It was only one bedroom and bath, and she could see the entire space from the doorway to her bedroom. At first glance, she didn't see anyone inside.

Pulse pounding, she returned to the kitchen and examined the envelope. No return address. No postage. Someone had hand delivered it and broken into her apartment to do so.

Her hand trembled as she ripped open the seal. A cry bubbled in her throat.

She removed the papers with a shaky hand. It was a copy of the log for signing out drugs in the ER.

According to the signature on the form, a signature that was a dead ringer for her own, she had signed out morphine and given it to Gloria Inman.

LIAM SPENT HALF the night reviewing his father's files on the Inman case and Jacob's on the fire. He'd been through them a dozen times already, but each time he hoped something would pop out and lead him to the answers.

Were the two connected?

They seemed to be. Then again, he and Jacob had chased the missing child angle with Cora's baby for so long and it hadn't been related to the fire, so he could be mistaken now.

But he had to pursue any lead that presented itself.

Five years had not lessened his need for the truth and justice for his father's death and the other lost lives.

He used a whiteboard to scribble the key components he'd identified and marked it off into categories. Facts, Suspects, Evidence, Leads, Motives.

He listed Inman's name and wrote *Wife's Death/Lawsuit* beneath it. Beneath the section labeled Motive, he scribbled the word *revenge*.

He added Peyton's name to the list of suspects. For motive, he wrote *Cover Up for Mistake in the ER?*

Although they had no proof there had actually been a mistake, much less that Peyton had caused it. Only hearsay that she might know who did.

He combed through the file again, focusing on an interview with the attending physician Dr. Butler. The doctor had seemed concerned about Inman's accusations and claimed he and the hospital staff had followed protocol and were not at fault. He denied any knowledge of the alleged conversation between Peyton and another staff member, and insisted Peyton was a topnotch nurse who prided herself on attention to detail.

Liam stood and stretched, then poured himself a scotch and returned to the files. He combed through interview after interview of the staff and studied Herbert Brantley's again. It sounded almost verbatim to what he'd told them today. Had he practiced what he was going to say? Was he lying?

Curious, he reviewed the lawsuit filed by Inman, then made a note of the prosecutor's name who'd represented Inman along with the hospital's attorney.

Bill Packard had represented Inman. Travis Ames the hospital. He sipped his scotch. Tomorrow he'd question them himself.

ANXIETY RIDDLED EVERY CELL in Peyton's body. Someone had been inside her apartment, and left paperwork
which pointed the finger at her for negligence in Mrs.
Inman's death.

She was being framed. Set up by whoever wanted
her to take the fall if the case went to court.

She laid the document on the kitchen table, grabbed
her flashlight from the laundry room and studied the
signature. It looked like hers, but she had not signed
out morphine or administered it to Gloria Inman that
night. Following protocol, she'd given the woman a shot
of epinephrine to jump-start her heart.

What in the world was going on?

She narrowed her eyes and checked the signature
again. Could a handwriting analyst be able to tell that
it had been forged?

Terrified of losing her license and her job and the
possibility of facing charges when her mother needed
her, she folded the paper, stuffed it back in the envelope and carried it to her bedroom. She had to hide it.
The desk maybe?

No, that was the first place someone would look.

The closet. She pulled out a shoebox full of old pho-
tographs and considered storing it in there but rethought
that idea.

Maybe she should just rip it up and throw it in the
trash. Or shred it in the shredder in the main office.

But what if someone caught her and asked questions?

Besides, if anyone learned about the papers and the
police confiscated them, they might actually help her.
That is, if the fingerprints of the person who'd put them
in her apartment were on the log sheet. If not...she'd
look guilty of giving Mrs. Inman an overdose.

After deciding she'd better hang on to the papers, she shoved them below her mattress.

The fact that someone had broken into her apartment made her skin crawl. She'd run away from Whistler to escape, yet whoever had set her up knew where she and her mother lived.

They'd probably been watching her all along.

Fear gripped her in its clutches, and she hurried to examine the locks on the windows and doors. The window locks and lock on the front door was untouched.

She checked the sliding glass doors and noted the lock on them was broken. A chill rippled through her, and she phoned Walter, the maintenance man, and asked him to replace her lock.

"You think someone broke in?" he asked.

"It looks that way. I'll report it to Fred, but I need a new lock tonight."

Although if the intruder had broken one lock, what would keep him from breaking a second?

While she waited for him to show, she pulled out a notepad. For five years now, she'd wondered what had gone wrong with Gloria Inman that night.

She scratched her head and began to jot down the names of each person she'd seen in the ER along with everyone who'd treated or worked on the woman.

The police had questioned them all back then.

But someone was hiding something. And the only way to clear her name was to figure out who was setting her up.

THE NEXT MORNING, Liam drove to Bill Packard's law office. Bill had represented Inman in the wrongful death lawsuit against the hospital.

Packard was late forties, silver at the temples, and dressed in a gray pin-striped suit. His secretary offered Liam coffee, and he accepted a cup, then joined Packard in his office. A state-of-the-art computer system occupied one corner in the sophisticated office which screamed money.

Liam flashed his credentials.

Packard steepled his hands on top of his cherrywood desk. "I don't understand. When you phoned, you told my secretary you wanted to discuss the Inman lawsuit. But that was settled five years ago."

"I'm aware of that," Liam said. "But as I'm sure you know, police never made an arrest regarding the arson at the hospital. Mr. Inman was a person of interest."

The attorney rubbed manicured fingers over his tie. "Yes, I know. Sheriff Maverick contacted me numerous times to ask if I knew Mr. Inman's whereabouts, but I told him I did not. And that is the truth."

"While you might not have been complicit in his disappearance, I still need to ask you some questions."

"I've been over this before with the sheriff," Mr. Packard said. "I don't have new information, so what is the point?"

"The point is that we found Mr. Inman and he's in custody." Liam fought irritation. "And I want to know who set the fire that killed my father and took multiple lives. So do the residents of Whistler."

Packard's jaw tightened. "If you're asking me to break attorney-client privilege, you understand that I can't, or I could be disbarred."

Liam expected as much. "Tell me this, Mr. Packard. Do you believe Mr. Inman started the fire?"

The attorney stood. "I can't answer that, and you know it. Now, are we done?"

Liam shook his head. "Not yet. According to the files, the judge threw out the case stating there was insufficient evidence. It also appears that you chose not to appeal or pursue the case. That tells me that you believed Mr. Inman's claims were unfounded."

"That doesn't tell you anything, except that there was insufficient evidence to pursue the case further." Packard sighed. "Now, you should go, Agent Maverick."

Liam stood, body tense. He believed in the system, but the attorney-client privilege aspect meant the lawyer could be covering for a murderer. And as a man of justice, that didn't sit well in his gut.

Travis Ames, the prosecutor for the case would no doubt pull the same argument. He needed to talk to someone who wasn't bound by the law.

According to Dr. Butler's deposition, the hospital had investigated and there was no wrongdoing on the part of the staff. But HIPAA laws prevented the man from divulging details of Mrs. Inman's medical treatment. And the fire had destroyed the files detailing her treatment in the ER.

PEYTON PACED HER KITCHEN while her coffee brewed. Last night, long after Fred installed a new lock on the sliding glass doors to her back patio and left her with a pole jammed at the bottom for her own sense of security, Peyton lay awake in the dark.

She had asked Fred to check around her mother's cottage during the night, then listened for sounds that her intruder had returned. Outside, the wind had howled off the mountains, and a tree branch scraped the windowpane.

She'd gotten up more than once to check to make sure someone hadn't broken in again.

Each time she closed her eyes, images of the night Gloria Inman died returned. The husband's fear. The chaos as the doctors worked to save her. The resident, Jody Plummer, who'd stepped in to assist. Herbert Brantley, the med tech who'd done the EKG. Herself, grabbing the medication from the tray to administer it into the IV.

When sleep finally came, it hadn't lasted long. The nightmare of the fire returned to haunt her. Her mother gasping for a breath. Dr. Butler performing CPR.

Dr. Butler showing her the paper that could have ruined her career.

He insisted he wanted to protect her and he'd saved her mother.

Her heart stuttered. Although as far as she knew, he was the only one who'd seen that paper. He'd supervised Gloria Inman's treatment.

Could he have made the mistake, then falsified the paperwork so he could blame her if Inman or another staff member pointed the finger at him?

Chapter Six

Peyton spent the morning on pins and needles while she made rounds with her patients. She pushed her mother outside in her wheelchair to have lunch in the garden. Soon winter would set in, and they'd have to stick to the indoor dining area, although the facility boasted a room with floor-to-ceiling windows to let in light and allow patients to enjoy the beautiful outdoor scenery while inside.

"Where did you run off to yesterday?" her mother asked as she sipped her sweet tea. "I missed you at lunch."

Peyton hadn't expected her to remember. "I had errands to do for the Gardens." They'd stopped discussing the fire years ago. She wanted her mother to focus on sweet memories, not the scariest one of her life.

"I'm so glad you're here with me," her mother said.

"Me, too, Mama." She intended to keep it that way. This morning she'd searched the news for the story on Barry Inman's arrest, but found nothing. The police were keeping it under wraps for some reason.

Perhaps until they had enough evidence to prove he set the fire.

She didn't know the man well enough to say whether

he was capable of arson and murder or not. Unless he hadn't meant for anyone to get hurt.

But that was impossible. A person who set fire to a hospital where there were critically ill and disabled patients would have to realize that everyone might not survive.

Her mother finished her chicken salad and took another sip of her tea. "You missed Val yesterday."

Peyton went still. Was her mother confused or had her sister found them?

Peyton wiped her mouth with her napkin. "What do you mean? I missed Val."

"Why, she came by when I was taking my afternoon nap. I woke up and there she was."

She'd thought her mother had been confused about the strange man showing up, but apparently there had been a man, the one who'd left that envelope in her apartment. Maybe her mother could describe him.

Maybe she was right about Val, too.

"Was Val here before or after the man came?" Peyton asked.

Her mother's brows pinched together. "What man, honey?"

Peyton gritted her teeth. "Yesterday you said a strange man came by and told you he left me something."

Worry knitted her mother's face, then confusion and frustration. "I...don't remember a man." She looked up into Peyton's eyes, searching. "What's wrong with me, Peyton? Why can't I remember things anymore?"

Peyton's heart broke. Once upon a time, her mother had been a strong, independent woman. Detail oriented.

She'd worked in a research medical lab analyzing rare virus strains for the CDC in Atlanta.

"Our memory gets shorter as we get older," Peyton said, giving her a version of the truth that her mother could handle. Broaching the words *Alzheimer's* or *dementia* or the fact that doctors suspected her mother had contracted one of those unnamed viruses and it had attacked her brain agitated her to the point where she had to be sedated. The first time they'd broached the possibility of a virus, her mother had insisted she needed to go to work and find a cure.

It was too late for that now.

"Mom, you said you saw Val yesterday. But we haven't seen her in three years, and you were sleeping. Could you have been dreaming?"

Irritation flashed in her mother's eyes. "Maybe it wasn't during my nap. It was…in the afternoon in the garden."

Peyton patted her mother's hand to keep her from becoming agitated. Although Leon said he'd seen a pretty young girl in the garden last night.

Had her sister found her and her mother?

LIAM CONSIDERED CALLING AHEAD for an appointment with Dr. Butler but decided not to give him a heads-up. If the man hadn't been truthful about Mrs. Inman's death, he'd had five years to perfect his lies.

And if he'd covered for another employee, Liam didn't want to give him time to alert the other person they were digging into the case again.

Unlike many of the doctors who'd worked at Whistler Hospital at the time of the fire, Dr. Butler had returned once the renovations had been completed. Many had transferred to other facilities during the interim.

At one point, Liam had considered leaving Whistler himself. Too many memories. But his roots ran deep, his family was here and he'd decided to stand up for the town in his father's name.

Getting justice was his top priority. No matter who he ticked off or what feathers he ruffled.

He parked at the hospital, and went inside, then headed to the chief of the hospital's office. A year ago, Dr. Butler had left the ER for administration. The receptionist, a cheerful middle-aged woman named Erma frowned when he flashed his credentials. "I need to speak to Dr. Butler."

"Can I ask what it's about?" Erma asked.

"The Barry Inman case and the fire five years ago." He locked his hands together in front of him. "It's important."

Alarm flashed in her eyes, and she pressed the speaker on her desk. "Dr. Butler, a Special Agent Liam Maverick is here to see you. He says it's important."

A slight pause, then the doctor wheezed a breath. "All right, send him in."

Erma walked him to the entry, then opened the door. Liam thanked her, quickly scanning the man's office as he entered. Files were stacked everywhere in a haphazard fashion. Sticky notes covered the edge of his desk by his computer and memos filled a cork bulletin board behind him. The bookshelves were a little neater with medical reference books along with books on hospital policies and management.

The doctor was late forties, neatly trimmed brown hair, medium height and build. In spite of the fact that he wasn't actively working the ER anymore, he wore a white doctor's lab coat over khakis and a button-down-collared shirt.

He stood and extended his hand, then gestured for Liam to sit. "You look familiar, Special Agent Maverick. And I recognize your last name. Have we met before?"

"Actually, you met my father during the investigation into the death of Gloria Inman. And my brother Jacob after the hospital fire." Liam had been working another case and had requested to come back to help with the fire investigation, but his boss had refused. He'd said Liam was too damn close to it. Liam had argued that was the reason he should work it.

But his boss hadn't budged.

"That's right. Those were both rough times."

"They were," Liam agreed. "I was surprised you returned to the hospital. So many people relocated and transferred."

Dr. Butler leaned back in his desk chair. "That's true. But I have roots in town, and after the devastation of the fire, I wanted to help rebuild the hospital. It felt like a betrayal to abandon a sinking ship."

Admirable, if that was true. A downside to being an agent meant Liam didn't quite trust anyone or accept their words at face value.

"Now, what brought you here today?" Dr. Butler asked. "Do you have a new lead on who set that fire?"

Liam adopted his poker face. "Barry Inman is in custody."

A slight flicker of the doctor's eyes indicated his surprise. "I realized the police suspected he set the fire to get revenge against the hospital. Did he finally confess?"

"As a matter of fact, he did not," Liam said. "He insists he's innocent. Which brings us back to the question, if anyone else had motive. Or if his story about Nurse Weiss held merit."

Dr. Butler shifted, his gaze dropping to his hands. When he looked up, his expression was flat. "As I told the sheriff, the hospital made no mistake that day. Mr. Inman must have misunderstood what he heard because he was looking for someone to blame."

Liam studied him. "I reviewed the files on Mr. Inman's case and know the charges were dropped. But there's no explanation. When the attorney for the hospital investigated Mr. Inman, which I assumed he did to prepare a defense, did he learn anything?"

Dr. Butler removed his glasses and rubbed a hand over his face. "He found nothing to incriminate one of the staff members."

It was the same story Dr. Butler had told five years ago.

"On the night of the fire, did you see anyone acting suspiciously in the hospital?" Liam asked.

Dr. Butler shook his head. "No. All I recall was that I was busy with a possible stroke patient, then the alarm sounded, and we had to move people outside."

"Nurse Weiss mentioned a homeless man who wandered into the ER seeking drugs. Do you remember seeing him?"

The doctor tilted his head to the side in thought. "Not specifically, but it's a common occurrence."

"She said security escorted him outside."

"That's not uncommon either. Occasionally one gets belligerent and we've had to call security."

Liam needed to look back at the security footage that

had been salvaged. Maybe the man was on camera. If he identified him, they'd have a chat. He also wanted to talk to the head of security. Jacob had questioned him already, but after five years, maybe he remembered something that hadn't stuck out at first.

"What about Nurse Weiss?" Liam asked. "What is your opinion of her?"

The man hesitated. "Peyton is a dedicated nurse. She's detail oriented, kind, compassionate and typically a good bridge between patients and families."

"Did she administer any drugs to Mrs. Inman?"

"Yes, of course. That was her job. I ordered epinephrine, which is Adrenalin, to jump-start the heart."

"Was it possible she gave the woman the wrong medication?"

A bead of sweat trickled down the side of the doctor's face. "I guess anything is possible, but Peyton is meticulous and checks the labels and the chart for allergies or other medications the patient is taking before she administers anything."

"But it was chaotic in the ER that night?"

"Yes, it was an unusually busy evening, and Mr. Inman was yelling at everyone. Security had to pull him from the room."

"He was afraid for his wife's life," Liam said.

Butler shifted again, obviously uncomfortable with the question.

"He was. I assured him we'd do everything we could, but I had to work on his wife and didn't have time to coddle him." He steepled his hands together. "But even on a chaotic night, safety protocol is followed to prevent mistakes. The staff logs every detail of the patient's treatment, including vitals and medications, as well as the amount and time administered."

"Did Nurse Weiss have a conversation with Mr. Inman?"

Butler scratched his head. "No, one of the other nurses did. Peyton was too busy."

So that eliminated the possibility that Inman had named her out of anger.

"How about the night of the fire? Did she act any differently that evening?"

Butler's brows pinched together. "Not that I recall. She helped evacuate patients, then was frantic to find her mother. Mrs. Weiss had gone into cardiac arrest, but I performed CPR and she survived."

Did Peyton feel indebted enough to him to lie or cover for him if he'd made the mistake in the ER with Gloria Inman?

WHILE HER MOTHER watched her favorite game show on TV, Peyton gathered her laundry. In the bedroom on the small corner desk though, she found an open photo album.

Photos of her and Valerie filled the pages. Memories washed over Peyton and made her chest clench. When they were little girls, they used to be so close. They'd played dolls together, braided each other's hair and snuggled together at night when Val got afraid of the dark.

But with age, they became more and more different. Val had jet-black hair, a model figure and looked exotic while Peyton felt like a plain Jane. But no matter how many compliments Val received or offers for dates, nothing seemed to make her happy. She became withdrawn and depressed. By fourteen, she was sneaking alcohol and drugs.

Their mother had forced her into rehab. For a while, her sister seemed to want to come clean. But six months later, she'd fallen off the wagon hard.

At eighteen, she'd run away. Peyton felt responsible. Val was her baby sister. She was supposed to take care of her. Save her.

But she'd failed.

She traced her finger over Val's face in the last Christmas photo they'd taken before Val ran away. Over the past ten years, she'd seen her sister three times. Each time, Val had returned, begging for money to get clean. Although each time, she'd accepted that money, used it for another fix, then disappeared.

Last year, she'd tried again, but Peyton had refused to give her money and offered to drive her to rehab instead. Val had become irate and belligerent and attacked her. Then she'd stolen Peyton's credit card and run.

Had she been in her mother's room the day before? Or in the gardens last night?

They didn't keep drugs in the patients' rooms but used a dispensary to ensure the medications were monitored. She tossed her mother's laundry into the washing machine, added soap and started it, then went to the living room.

"Mom, I have to go back to work. I'll see you this evening."

Her mother barely looked up from her game show but smiled when Peyton dropped a kiss on her cheek. A bad premonition enveloped her as she left, and she hurried outside to go to the pharmacy.

If her sister had shown up here, it couldn't be good.

AFTER LEAVING THE HOSPITAL, Liam stopped by Jacob's office. Together they reviewed security footage from the hospital the night of the fire. They had both studied it numerous times, but today he was looking for the drug seeker. A few minutes into the footage, he found it.

"What makes you suspicious of this guy?" Jacob asked.

Liam shrugged. "Peyton mentioned him, said security escorted him out. What if he was in a bad place, wanted drugs and set the fire so he could steal some from the pharmacy?"

Jacob hissed. "We were so preoccupied with the theory that the person who kidnapped Cora's baby started the fire, that we didn't pursue other leads."

"It may not be related but I'm going to follow through," Liam said. "I'll show the footage to Peyton and see if she recognizes the man. And I'll have the analyst at the Bureau run the man's face through facial rec and look for a name." Could the answer be as simple as a junkie trying to steal drugs?

Jacob nodded. "I'll see if I can locate the pharmacist on duty that night. He might know if any drugs went missing or if someone tried to break into the room where they store the medications."

Liam headed out to his vehicle with the footage. Peyton claimed to have told him everything she knew the day before, but his gut instincts warned him she was holding back, that she might be the key to unraveling the mystery.

His phone buzzed as he climbed in his car. An unknown number appeared on his screen. He answered, "Special Agent Maverick."

A woman's voice, a low, strained whisper. "You were at the hospital asking about Barry Inman today."

Liam tensed. "I was. Do you have information about him?"

"Barry Inman cheated on his wife."

"Who is this?" Liam asked.

But the line went dead in his hands.

Anger railed inside Liam as the implications set in. The police should have known about the affair. If Inman had reason to kill his wife, it gave him motive for murder.

Had Inman killed his wife so he could move on with his lover? If so, why file a lawsuit against the hospital? It didn't make sense.

He started the engine and peeled from the parking lot. He'd sensed Peyton had been hiding something. He was going to find out what the hell it was.

Chapter Seven

Using his hands-free device, Liam phoned Jacob and described his interaction with Dr. Butler as he drove toward Golden Gardens. "I just received an anonymous call from a woman who claims Barry Inman was having an affair."

"Really?" Jacob muttered a curse. "That's interesting. And could provide Inman's motive for killing his wife."

"Exactly," Liam agreed. "If Inman wanted to get rid of his wife, he could have done something to have caused her heart attack. Or if he tried to end the affair and his mistress was unhappy about his decision, she would have had motive for murder."

"You may be onto something," Jacob said.

"What did the autopsy say was Mrs. Inman's cause of death?" Liam asked.

"Cardiac arrest," Jacob replied.

"Do you have the toxicology report?"

"Hang on. Let me look in the file." Liam veered onto the highway leading to River's Edge. Late-afternoon shadows flickered across the road, tree branches bobbing in the wind as he passed farmland and houses scattered here and there.

Jacob grunted. "You won't believe this, Liam, but I can't find a toxicology report."

"That can't be right," Liam said. "The attorneys would have needed that information." If he couldn't get hold of it, he might request an exhumation of Mrs. Inman's body and another autopsy performed. "Who was the ME?"

"Dr. Hammerhead."

"I'll give him a call. He should have kept a copy."

Jacob grunted. "Sounds like a plan. I'll question Inman about the affair and find out the woman's name. This could change everything."

Theories rattled around in Liam's head. If negligence was involved in Mrs. Inman's death, and someone wanted to cover it up, a fire would have achieved that purpose. A jilted lover or a husband wanting out of his marriage was also another viable theory.

"Did you question Inman's family and neighbors about the couple's marriage?"

The sound of Jacob turning pages echoed over the line. "Dad did. According to his notes, the woman who lived across the street claimed the couple argued sometimes, and Inman was gone a lot, but there were never any domestic disputes. Lady who lived next door said Mrs. Inman shopped all the time, and the couple fought about money. But she never saw anything to make her believe Inman would hurt his wife." Jacob paused. "Inman's own mother, Gwen, insisted her son loved his wife and was distraught over her death to the point that she feared he might be suicidal."

"Follow up with all of them and see if they were aware of this alleged affair."

"On it. Will keep you posted."

"Same here." Liam ended the call, then phoned the ME's office and asked to speak to Dr. Hammerhead. His receptionist said he was in a meeting and agreed to have him call Liam ASAP.

Liam hung up, then maneuvered the switchbacks on the mountain road until he reached Golden Gardens. He stopped at the security gate and identified himself, then pulled through the open gate and drove toward Peyton's place.

When he arrived, her car was parked in front of her apartment. He veered into an empty spot, climbed out, walked up the sidewalk to her door, rang the doorbell and waited, but no one answered. Inside, the lights were off.

He returned to his vehicle, then punched her number. She didn't answer her phone either, so he left a message that he was waiting at her place and they needed to talk.

"HAVE YOU SEEN any strangers in here at the pharmacy?" Peyton asked Owen, the resident pharmacist who manned the drug dispensary.

Owen narrowed his eyes. "No."

"And no drugs have gone missing?"

He shook his head. "What's going on? Why are you asking about missing drugs?"

"I was just checking. I think someone may have been inside my apartment yesterday and thought maybe you'd seen someone lurking around here."

"Did you report this to the director?"

"I did, and I had my locks changed."

"I'll keep an eye out, Peyton. Thanks for the heads-up." He stepped from the room, locked the door, then set the code. Each of the nurses and the staff doctor, who made weekly rounds and was on call, had the code and could check out medications when needed.

They walked down the hallway together, and Owen exited the building. Peyton scanned the corridors, but she had the odd sense that someone was watching her as she hurried outside. Needing the exercise and fresh air to help alleviate her anxiety, she'd walked to the cottages this morning. But with night shadows already falling and dark storm clouds rolling in, the mountains looked ominous and eerie.

She walked past the gardens to cut across the property to her apartment. The trees shivered in the wind, leaves raining down. Her shoes crunched dead leaves and brush as she scanned the gardens in case Leon, or the mysterious alleged girl, maybe Val, was visiting again.

The resident cat who liked to roam the property appeared, his black coat hardly visible in the shadows, although his bright green eyes glowed as he paused to stare up at her. "Hey, Kitty," she murmured as she approached the furball.

He appeared to be limping, so she crept closer. A second later, he scrambled away and disappeared into the edge of the woods with a screech. Worried he was injured, she inched toward the thicket of trees, and saw him racing up a tree. He couldn't be injured badly to climb.

She turned to head back to her place, but suddenly two hands grabbed her and pushed her against a tree. She tried to scream, but a hand clamped down over her mouth, then she looked into the crazed eyes of her sister.

Her eyes were dazed, wild looking, and her hands held Peyton firmly.

"You have to help me, sis."

Peyton's heart raced, but she gave a little nod so Val would release her. As soon as she did, she stepped away from her and threw up a warning hand.

"Mom said she saw you," Peyton said. "Why are you here, Val? You want money or drugs?"

Val's eyes filled with tears. "I'm in trouble. Someone's after me, Peyton."

Peyton's heart stuttered with fear. Although reality crashed back. Her sister had lied to her so many times. "Your drug dealer. How much do you owe him?"

"It's not him," Val said in a choked whisper.

Peyton gritted her teeth. She'd been down this road so many times. "I can't help you, Val." She turned to walk away. "And stay away from Mama. She doesn't need your crap."

She had taken two steps when her sister jumped her from behind and shoved her to the ground. Peyton's face hit the leaves and she tasted dirt and blood as she bit her tongue.

"I'm your sister—you can't desert me," Val cried as she shook her. "Stop running and listen to me."

"Why? So, you can give me the same old excuses."

Peyton rolled sideways in an attempt to flip her sister to her back but failed.

Suddenly a light flickered across the yard, and a voice called out, asking who was there.

Val jumped up and ran into the woods, leaving Peyton disoriented and bleeding on the ground.

LIAM WAS JUST about to call Peyton again when she stumbled around the side of the building to the front door.

The wind whipped her hair around her face, and she

was holding her hand over one cheek. She wavered as she walked.

His instincts jumped to full alert. Something was wrong. She was hurt.

She swayed again, then made it to the front door and fumbled with her key.

He slid from his car, closed the door and walked up the path to her apartment. By the time he reached her, she'd stooped down and was searching for her keys in the grass.

"Ms. Weiss?"

She startled and jerked her head around, eyes wide and wary.

He held out a hand to let her know he meant no harm. "Are you all right?"

She rasped out a breath. "I dropped my keys, that's all."

That was not all. Blood dotted her lip, and her cheek looked swollen as if someone had hit her.

He pulled a penlight from his pocket and shone it on the ground. He spotted the keys, then reached into the bush in front of her stoop and snagged them. She started to stand but swayed again and he caught her arm to steady her.

A tear slipped down her cheek and lingered.

He didn't speak, simply unlocked the door for her. She averted her gaze and stepped inside.

He didn't wait on an invitation. He followed her. "What happened?"

Her eyes flickered with a look he didn't quite understand. Fear? Worry? Secrets again.

He dropped her keys on the table by the door and trailed her into the living area.

"I tripped and fell." She turned to face him, arms folded across her chest. "What are you doing here?"

"I need to ask you some more questions." Although the sight of her battered face raised his protective instincts, and he softened toward her. He stepped closer, removed a handkerchief from his pocket and lifted it to her lip to wipe away the blood.

She sucked in a sharp breath but caught his hand with hers as if his gesture was crossing the line into an intimacy she didn't welcome. "Excuse me—let me clean up a bit."

Without waiting for a response, she fled down the hall, ducked into the bathroom and shut the door. He heard the water running, then walked over to the refrigerator, found a cloth in a drawer and made her an ice pack.

While he waited, he glanced around her apartment. A decent blue sofa and comfortable club chair, farmhouse table, and a small fireplace gave the room a cozy feel. Nothing fancy or expensive indicating she'd accepted a bribe.

A photograph on the mantel drew his eyes, and he studied it. A woman with brown hair held two little girls on her lap. The picture had to have been taken years ago because Peyton looked to be about ten years old. The little girl beside her had jet-black hair, ivory skin and huge dark eyes.

Peyton's sister?

The sound of footsteps made him jerk his head around, and Peyton entered the living area. She'd cleaned her lip and face, but she was going to have a shiner.

"What are you doing?" Anger laced her tone as if she didn't like him looking at her personal pictures.

"Waiting on you." He gestured toward the photograph. "Is that your sister?"

Her jaw tightened. "It was. She's dead now."

"I'm sorry. I didn't mean to pry."

"That's what you do, isn't it?"

This time belligerence. Under the circumstances though, he ignored the jab. Instead he offered the ice pack to her. "It'll help with the swelling."

She blinked and looked away but accepted the ice pack and pressed it to her cheek.

"What happened?" he asked again.

"I told you. I tripped and fell." She walked over to the fireplace, lit the gas logs, then sank into the club chair beside the fire. Her body trembled as she pulled an afghan over her.

"It looks more like you had a run-in with someone's fist."

She winced and averted her gaze again. "I saw the resident cat by the gardens. He was limping and ran into the woods. I thought he was hurt so I chased him, but it was dark, and I tripped over a tree root. Face-planted into a rock," she said as if daring him not to believe her.

While her story had a ring of truth to it, she was leaving something out.

"Do any of your patients ever get violent?"

She shrugged. "Not any of mine," she said. "Now, what are you doing here tonight, Agent Maverick? I answered all of your questions yesterday."

Liam decided she wasn't going to change her story, so he let the question about her so-called accident go for the moment. "I heard something about Barry Inman and wanted to run it by you."

She lowered the ice pack and set it on the table. Her cheek was bright red from the cold and the impact of whatever had struck her. For a second, she looked so young and vulnerable and innocent that he was tempted to pull her into his arms.

Get a grip, man. She was a suspect. Or perhaps a witness who was withholding information in the most important case of Liam's life, his father's murder.

She ran her fingers through her long wavy hair and plucked a crumbled leaf from the strands. "What are you talking about?"

"I received a tip saying that Barry Inman had had an affair. Do you know anything about that?"

A frown pinched her face. "No. The only time I met the man was when he rushed into the ER with his wife."

"Was the wife alert when she was brought in?"

"Not really. She faded in and out of consciousness and complained of chest pains."

"How did the couple seem together?"

She rolled her eyes. "Just as you'd expect when someone's having a heart attack. Panicked and afraid."

"No arguments?"

She leaned forward, then twisted her mouth in thought. "Agent Maverick, the woman was in critical condition. Her husband was distraught. That's all I can tell you."

"So, you didn't think he acted suspicious, as if he'd hurt her?"

Peyton's eyes widened. "You think Mr. Inman was responsible for his wife's death?"

"I don't know," Liam said. "But we have to explore

every possibility. If Mr. Inman was having an affair and wanted out of the marriage, he would have had motive. Or if his lover wanted him to leave his wife and he refused, she might have wanted Mrs. Inman dead."

Shock streaked Peyton's face.

"Did you see a strange woman lurking in the waiting room or anywhere near the ER?"

Peyton rubbed her temple. "Not that I recall, although there were several people in the waiting room and other patients in the ER. At one point, Barry was on the phone in the hall. He was pacing and seemed agitated, but I thought he was just worried about his wife."

"Do you know who he was talking to?"

She shook her head.

He'd have Bennett request phone records. If his lover was on the phone, they could have planned Gloria Inman's death together.

Chapter Eight

Peyton struggled to contain her anxiety at the way the agent's gaze kept lingering on her face. He knew she was lying.

But she didn't intend to share her personal problems with the man. Her sister's drug issues had nothing to do with the reason he was here. Having him see the bruise on her face was humiliating enough without admitting that she'd failed to save her sister from a life on the streets.

His phone buzzed and he excused himself to answer it. She stared into the fire, her sister's angry face etched in her mind. Maybe she should have told Val to come back to her place, that they could talk. She might be able to convince her to enter rehab again. Maybe this time it would work.

Her heart gave a pang. She'd been down that road so many times and ended up with the same result. It broke her every time.

The agent ended the call, then walked back to her chair. "My analyst texted a copy of a piece of the security footage from the night of the fire. He's been looking for anyone suspicious, and also any commonality between that night and the night Inman's wife died. You mentioned seeing a man who appeared to be homeless seeking drugs."

She rubbed at the scrape on her knuckle from where she'd hit the ground earlier. "Yes."

"Take a look at it. Tell me if there's anyone you recognize or anyone who stands out."

He removed a small tablet from inside his jacket, accessed the footage and angled it for her to see. First was footage of the ER the night Mrs. Inman died. Peyton watched as Barry Inman rushed in beside his wife. Barry looked shocked and terrified and Gloria was gasping for breath.

Two other people entered and went to the admissions desk. Another ambulance raced up and medics wheeled a pregnant woman inside. Then the man she'd thought was homeless. He wore a worn black hoodie, jeans and kept his head down as he approached the desk.

"Was that the man you mentioned?" the agent asked.

Peyton nodded. "You can see the nurse behind the desk looking at her computer. She must have recognized his face or name." A second later, she called the security guard who appeared and escorted the man from the ER. He looked unsteady on his feet and jerked his arm away when he got outside.

She continued watching until the agent paused on a woman who entered wearing a dark raincoat and hat. Her head was bent, and she avoided looking at the camera. Her posture and rushed movements indicated she was nervous, and she gripped her phone and spoke into it as she ducked into the ladies' room. Five minutes later, she exited the bathroom and hurried outside.

"If Inman had an affair, that could have been his lover," the agent pointed out. "Do you recognize her?"

Peyton shook her head. "You can't even see her face."

The agent switched to show footage of the night of the fire. She watched people enter and be taken to the ER rooms, and two people who were discharged.

No sign of Barry Inman or the woman in the dark raincoat. Although another woman entered, her face shielded by a thick wool scarf.

She checked all around her as if she was afraid of something, then she hesitated for a second as she bypassed the waiting room and slipped down the hall.

"Do you know who that is?" the agent asked.

She shook her head, but one of the cameras caught a quick flash of the woman's face.

Dear God. Peyton went still. The girl wearing the scarf was Val.

UNEASE DARKENED PEYTON'S EYES. What the hell was she hiding?

"Do you recognize that woman?" Liam asked.

She shook her head, but her breath sounded shaky. "If I'd seen something suspicious, I would have told you, Agent Maverick." She stood. "Now it's been a long day and I'm exhausted."

The tension emanating from her was palpable. He had the urge to draw her into his arms and assure her everything would be all right. Although how could he do that when he was almost certain she was lying again?

"My analyst also learned the name of the drug seeker. When he was turned away from Whistler Hospital that night, he hit up an urgent care. He was found later and had OD'd in an alley." So that was a dead end.

"I'm sorry," Peyton said. "Drug problems, especially opioids, are rampant now."

His phone buzzed. Jacob. "If you think of anything that can help, please give me a call."

Peyton's gaze locked with his for a moment. The wariness in her eyes troubled him. So did that damn bruise on her face. Made him want to comfort her. Promise her that if she was holding something back and was too frightened to talk, he'd protect her.

If she hadn't fallen and he was right, someone had punched her.

A boyfriend? Lover? Another employee? A patient?

Dammit. Why would she cover for him?

"Peyton," he said, as he paused at the door. "If you're in trouble, I can help."

A pained, frightened look darkened her eyes, then her lips curved into a forced smile. "Thank you, Agent Maverick. But I'm fine."

He didn't believe her for a minute. She opened the door and scanned the lawn and parking lot as if she was looking for someone.

He stepped outside and did the same.

Worry knotted his belly. She was scared. Of what, he wasn't sure. But fear rolled off of her in waves.

His father's mantra—Respect and Protect—echoed in his head. It was one reason he and his brothers had all chosen to become first responders. Another reason had been to honor their father's memory.

His gut instinct shouted that Peyton Weiss needed his help and protection. But she was either too full of pride or terrified of something to ask for it.

"I meant what I said—call me if you need anything," he murmured as his dark gaze locked with hers. "Any time night or day."

She clamped her teeth over her lower lip, gave a little nod, then shut the door. He scanned the property as he walked back to his car. Everything seemed quiet.

Still, his gut told him Peyton needed a friend as he climbed into his car. His phone buzzed with a text. It was from Jacob.

Inman gave up the name of the woman he had affair with. Sondra Evans. Claims it was over, that he broke it off.

Liam responded with, Her contact info?
Jacob texted back an address.

Liam: I'm not too far from there now. Will swing by and talk to her.

Jacob: Thanks. Inman insists she had nothing to do with his wife's death. Let me know your take.

Liam: Copy that.

Liam pressed the accelerator and headed toward Sondra Evans's house. All along they'd assumed Inman's wife's death was connected to the fire. But if Gloria Inman had been killed by her husband's lover or ex, it was possible they were unrelated.

Which put them back to square one. Then who had set the fire and why?

If Inman or Evans had killed Gloria, why would Inman have brought attention to her death with a lawsuit? That didn't make sense. Unless Evans had killed the wife and Inman had no idea...

He'd drill Sondra Evans for the answers.

PARANOIA BUILT INSIDE PEYTON. She'd had no idea her sister had been at the hospital the night of the fire.

Had Val come to visit her mother? Or had she been there for another reason? Was she seeking drugs?

Tears blurred her eyes as she pressed a hand to her aching cheek. How had things gone so wrong with her sister? Many addicts turned to drugs or alcohol because of a trauma in their past. But as far as she knew, Val hadn't been involved in an accident, or been the victim of a violent attack or abuse.

Dark thoughts entered her mind about Val's motive, thoughts she didn't want to entertain. The fire had started in a storage closet next to the records room. One of the pharmacy rooms storing drugs was located across the hall.

She closed her eyes and willed away the terror gripping her. Her sister was an addict, and she had stolen from her and her mother, but she wouldn't set a fire as a diversion in order to break into the drugs cabinet.

Would she?

God, please no…

Peyton walked to the sliders, opened the curtain and peered outside. Regret for not listening to Val haunted her.

Tears blurred her eyes, and she searched the darkness. Was her sister lurking in the shadows waiting to show herself again? Would she try to break in during the night?

She phoned Fred, the head of security. "Please check around my mother's cottage during the night. I thought I saw someone lurking out there earlier."

"I'll go right now and have Bobby swing by every hour."

"Thanks. And Fred, tomorrow I'd like to look at the security footage near my mom's place and for the gardens. I don't like the fact that Mom said she saw a stranger in her room."

"Are you sure she really saw someone? I hate to mention it, but she's starting to see things. I tried talking to her a few times, and she forgot who I was."

Pain tightened Peyton's chest. "I know, but it's better to be safe than sorry."

He said softly that he would, and they agreed to meet in the morning, then they ended the call. The envelope in Peyton's apartment proved her mother hadn't imagined this man. He'd visited her mother as a warning to her. A reminder to keep her silence.

A movement near the bushes to the right caught her eye. She gripped the edge of the slider, her heart hammering as she watched. There it was again, just a flicker of something moving behind the bushes. Then it darted through the trees and disappeared.

She watched and waited, fear tightening her shoulder blades. Was Val out there? Had she seen Agent Maverick at her door?

She claimed someone was after her. Peyton assumed it was her drug dealer or someone she owed money.

A screeching noise echoed from outside. Peyton went still, searching the yard and woods beyond. The screech grew louder. Was it the wind whistling off the mountain? Or…someone who was hurt? One of the patients? Leon again?

Suddenly another movement, a shadow traveling toward her deck. She grabbed the fire poker by the fireplace and braced it to use as a weapon. The screech again.

Her breath caught, then puffed out as the resident cat lumbered into sight on her back patio. Just as she'd thought, he was limping. Her heart ached for him, and she removed the stick at the bottom of the door, then opened the sliders.

"Come here, buddy," she murmured as she stooped to pick him up. If he was injured, she had to nurse him back to health. She lifted her hand and stroked his fur. "It's okay, bud, you can stay with me tonight."

Just before she scooped him into her arms, she sensed someone approaching from behind her. Then something hard struck her head. Pain splintered her skull. The world tilted and spun. Stars danced in front of her eyes.

Then the world went black.

Chapter Nine

Liam couldn't shake the premonition that Peyton was in trouble as he parked at Sondra Evans's town house in the hills of Pine Ridge. The townhomes looked fairly new and well-kept and boasted a walking trail around the man-made lake which attracted residents to the development.

Jacob had sent him background information on the woman. The thirty-four-year-old University of North Carolina graduate worked as a sales rep for a pharmaceutical company where she'd met Barry Inman, who had trained her on the job.

The lawns were well maintained, the brick fronts all consistent. He found Sondra's unit, hurried to the door and rang the bell. A minute later, he heard her voice from inside.

"Our neighborhood has a no-soliciting policy," she said curtly.

Liam glanced down at his slacks and button-down shirt. He hadn't realized he looked like a salesman. "I'm not selling anything," he said, then flashed his badge. "My name is Special Agent Liam Maverick. I need to talk to you."

A minute passed, and he thought she was going to

decline, but she opened the door. "You're a federal agent? What is this about?"

Liam gestured toward the entryway. "Ma'am, can I come in? I'm not sure you want to discuss this on your doorstep."

A debate warred in her eyes. Should she let him in or risk the consequences of not cooperating? She relented and stepped outside, then led him through the foyer to a den with leather furniture.

She gestured toward the wing chair and he sat, then waited on her to do the same. "What's this about?"

"We recently located Barry Inman and brought him in for questioning regarding the Whistler Hospital fire five years ago."

She swallowed and glanced down at her manicured hands. "I saw the news. You think he set the fire because of that lawsuit."

"That's what I'm trying to figure out."

She lifted her head and looked at him. "I don't know how I can help."

Liam adopted a casual position. "You worked with Mr. Inman, correct?"

She gave a little nod. "Barry trained me at the pharmaceutical company."

"How would you describe your relationship?"

She shifted and crossed her legs. "We were business colleagues. Barry taught me a lot about the business, and I was grateful for that."

Liam arched a brow. "Grateful enough to sleep with him?"

Anger flashed across her face. "If you're implying Barry pressured me or there was sexual harassment involved, you're way off base."

Liam raised a brow. She was certainly defensive of the man. "Then enlighten me. I know you had an affair. Were you in love with him?"

Her breath hissed out. "I don't see how that's any of your business."

Liam leaned forward. "It's my business because his wife died under suspicious circumstances, and he's a suspect in an arson/homicide investigation."

"It was just one night," she said in a low voice. "He was upset because he'd lost a big client and we were working late. We had too much to drink." She shrugged. "It just happened. You understand?"

"But you wanted it to happen again?"

She jiggled her leg up and down. "I was attracted to Barry, and he was a nice man. But he was married, and he loved his wife."

"How did you feel about his rejection?"

She cut her eyes away from him. "It wasn't a rejection. We both agreed it was a mistake. He wanted to preserve his marriage, and we decided it wouldn't happen again."

But she wanted more. He sensed it the way she looked down at her hands, in the way her voice quivered.

A strained silence fell between them. He hoped she would fill it, but she seemed to clam up completely.

"Did you see or talk to Barry the night his wife died?"

She shook her head a little too vigorously.

"How about the night of the fire? Where were you?"

"I'd just flown back home after a business trip. I went straight home and to bed."

"Alone or were you seeing Barry?"

Her mouth worked as she struggled with her reply. "Alone. I told you we broke it off."

But she had no solid alibi.

She and Barry both had access to narcotics and other drugs through their work. He wanted to see that toxicology report. Perhaps the hospital hadn't made a mistake.

Barry or Sondra might have murdered Gloria Inman.

PEYTON'S HEAD POUNDED as if someone was beating her skull with a hammer. She slowly opened her eyes, wincing as she realized she was lying on her back patio. The memory of being assaulted returned, and nausea rose to her throat.

Had Val come back and attacked her?

Or was it the man who'd threatened her?

Drawing in a breath to stem the nausea, she pushed herself to a sitting position. The land swayed, trees dipping and moving. The wind swirled dead leaves around her, blowing them inside through her sliders which were still open.

Choking back a sob, she glanced across the backyard, but didn't see her sister or anyone else. Pushing up on shaky legs, she clawed at the door edge to steady herself and then stumbled inside. Wind howled through the open door and she pulled it shut, then turned to see if someone was in the apartment.

Pausing to listen, she held her breath and strained her ears for sounds of an intruder. A voice? Footsteps?

Nothing except for the ticking of the wall clock above the fireplace. Midnight. She'd been unconscious for over an hour.

She lifted her hand to the back of her head and felt sticky blood matted in her hair. She jammed the pole back into the doorframe and locked the sliders, then heard a sound. A low cry.

Val? Or…no, the cat.

Was he hurt? Was the intruder still inside?

Grabbing the fire poker again, she inched through the apartment, bracing for another attack. But she didn't see anyone inside.

Her breath whooshed out, and she forgot about her throbbing head and went in search of the cat. Still dizzy, she gripped the wall edge until she felt steadier on her feet. In the kitchen, she found him hiding beneath the table.

Stooping down, she called his name. "Come here, Kitty. Come on, I won't hurt you."

Typically he came to her, but tonight his back was curled up, his hair standing on end.

"Looks like we've both had a rough day," she muttered. She stood and retrieved the small bag of cat food she kept on hand from her pantry. He'd never ventured inside before, but she'd left food on the back deck. She poured a small handful into the bowl, then shook it and set it at the edge of the table on the floor.

Slowly he inched his way toward the bowl. She dropped down beside him and stroked his fur gently as he nibbled at the food. When he'd eaten a little, she picked him up and cradled him to her, then examined his paw. He was limping earlier, and he winced when she touched it. He had put some weight on it, so she didn't think it was broken. And she didn't find blood or see any cuts. If he wasn't better in a day or two, she'd take him to the vet.

For now, she'd let him sleep and see if he felt better in the morning.

She settled him on a blanket at the foot of her bed and went to examine her own injuries. God, she looked battered and bruised.

Two attacks in one day.

She itched to call the police and report this one.

But what if it had been Val? Could she turn her sister in to the police?

LIAM'S PHONE WOKE him up at six in the morning. He rolled over and rubbed his bleary eyes. He'd barely slept for thinking about the case.

Peyton's battered face haunted him. What had happened to her and why had she lied?

His phone dinged again. He snatched it and saw it was his partner, Bennett. "Maverick."

"I've been running various programs to compare employees who worked at the Whistler Hospital with employees from other hospitals close by, looking for any instances of misconduct, wrongful death or suspicious deaths and fires."

"Go on."

"Anyway, I didn't find any instances of arson, but I did some cases where patients died suddenly, and the families questioned the deaths. Two at Pine Ridge Hospital, Edna Fouts and Lydia Corgin. The third, Hilda Rogers, died at a nursing home called Serenity Now. I'll send what I dug up so far on them."

"People are lawsuit happy these days," Liam said. "What happened in the cases?"

"They were dropped. I did some digging and it turned out they shared one thing in common. The same Physician's assistant."

Liam's heart hammered. "Do you have a name?"

"Miller Conrad." A pause. "He was also on duty at Whistler Hospital the night Gloria Inman died."

Liam's instincts kicked in, and he threw his legs over

the side of the bed. "Send me his contact information. I'll have a chat with him."

"On its way."

Liam shuffled toward the shower. If there was a link between Gloria Inman's death and this PA, he'd find it.

Thirty minutes later, he wolfed down a breakfast sandwich, poured a travel mug full of coffee and headed out to his vehicle. Bennett had sent Conrad's work schedule. It was the man's day off, so Liam swung by his place.

He lived on the mountain in an older clapboard house that looked in disrepair. When Liam parked and got out, two big dogs ran up to him. He paused to let the dogs sniff him and to scratch their backs.

Before he made it to the door, it opened and a stocky guy with a goatee stepped outside.

He spotted Liam and his car and stopped, his brows climbing his forehead.

"Mr. Conrad." Liam flashed his badge and identified himself. "I need to talk to you."

"It'll have to wait," Conrad said. "I have to get my mother breakfast. She's bedridden."

The hair on the back of Liam's neck prickled just as it always did when he felt something was off. "No problem. I'll come in and wait."

Panic flared on the man's face, then he turned and rushed inside, slamming the door behind him.

PEYTON WOKE TO the sound of the kitty purring. She rolled over and rubbed his back and he snuggled up to her.

"You're a sweetie," she said softly. He reminded her of the cat she and Val had had growing up. "If you're going to stay with me, I'll have to buy you a litter box." Although as soon as she said it, he hopped down. She slipped from bed and followed him. He lumbered straight to the sliders and scratched at the door.

"So that's the way it's going to be. You like your independence, don't you?" She understood. She'd been alone a long time herself.

She knelt and scratched his neck again, then opened the curtain and glanced at the backyard. Last night someone had attacked her on her patio. But once they'd knocked her unconscious, they'd disappeared.

Why? Nothing had been taken. If it was the person who'd threatened her, why hadn't he just killed her? Did he just want to toy with her, keep her living in fear?

She unlocked the door and let the kitty outside. "Come back tonight," she whispered as he scrambled off toward the gardens. "Maybe we can be friends."

She closed and locked the door, then rubbed at her temple. Her head was throbbing, so she downed some painkillers and showered. Last night, after cleaning up the blood, she'd felt a lump starting to form. Today the lump was still there, so she styled her hair to make sure it wasn't exposed and left it loose around her shoulders instead of the ponytail she usually wore to work.

By the time she finished her coffee and ate a piece of toast, her phone was ringing. She rushed to get it and saw it was Joanna, so she punched Connect.

"Peyton, you need to come to your mom's. I stopped by to give her her morning meds and found her unconscious. The medics are here now."

Peyton's breath stalled in her chest. "I'll be right there." Panic stabbed at her as she grabbed her keys and ran for the door.

Chapter Ten

"Mr. Conrad?" Liam said as he pushed open the door.

"I'm sorry—I need to tend to my mother." A low groan sounded from the rear of the house, and Conrad disappeared down the hallway.

Liam quickly scanned the small den and kitchen. The place was a mess with dishes stacked everywhere and laundry piled in a chair in the corner. The groaning noise echoed again, and he headed down the hall.

Was someone hurt inside? Was that why the man had shut the door in his face?

He passed a small, cluttered office, then noted two bedrooms at the end of the hall. The scent of antiseptic and an acrid odor filled the air, one that smelled like death.

Senses alert, he glanced to the left. A bedroom that looked just as cluttered as the rest of the house. To the right, he spotted Conrad injecting something into an IV that hung on a pole by the bed. The strong smell of medication and sickness permeated the space. Prescription medications lined a stainless-steel rolling cart against the wall.

"It's okay, Mama," Conrad said. "I know you're in pain, but the medication should kick in soon."

Liam watched, his stomach churning as Conrad picked up a glass of water and helped his mother take a sip through a straw. The sight of the frail, ghostly pale woman twisted at his insides. Her hair was gray and thin, her bones poking through her skin. Blue veins stood out on her wiry arms in a crisscross pattern and age spots dotted her leathery hands.

Liam cleared his throat, and Conrad glanced over his shoulder at him, a pained expression on his face.

"Do you need help?" Liam asked. "An ambulance?"

Conrad shook his head no, then covered his mother with a blanket and patted her shoulder. "Rest now, Mama. I'll be back to check on you in a little bit."

He glared at Liam, then motioned for him to leave the room. Liam studied the woman, searching for signs of elder abuse, but didn't see any visible injuries. And Conrad had been gentle with her.

"Are you okay, Ma'am?" he asked gruffly.

Perspiration beaded her forehead and her eyes were glassy with pain and medication. But she muttered something like her son was a good boy.

A vein throbbed in Conrad's neck, and he pointed down the hall with a sharp look, clearly angry that Liam had invaded his mother's bedroom.

Liam led the way back to the living room and to the front door. But Liam refused to be dismissed.

"Mr. Conrad, your mother is obviously very ill. Don't you think she should be at the hospital?"

The man scrubbed a hand over his face. "There's nothing else they can do," he said in a pained voice. "She's final stages, ovarian cancer. She fought it for as long as she could, but the last chemo wiped her out, and the cancer spread to her bones. All the doctors can do now is to make her comfortable."

Liam couldn't imagine watching your loved one die a slow and painful death. "I'm sorry to hear that. It must be difficult."

He made a low sound in his throat. "You'd think I'd be used to seeing death and dying on the job, but it still gets to me."

"It's different when it's your own family," Liam said, sympathy nudging at his suspicions.

"Anyway," Conrad said. "What are you doing here?"

Liam explained about his investigation. "I'm talking to everyone who was on duty the night Mrs. Inman died."

Conrad heaved a breath. "I was working that night, although I didn't see anything out of the ordinary. Except the man blew up when his wife died."

"Blew up?"

"Yeah, I thought he was going to attack the doctor and Nurse Weiss."

They hadn't mentioned that they'd felt physically threatened. "Inman claims he heard Nurse Weiss say something about a mistake in the ER. Did she talk to you about that?"

Conrad shook his head. "No, but it was a madhouse all evening. One emergency after another."

"What about the night of the fire? Did you see Mr. Inman in the hospital?"

Another shake of his head. "Sorry, I'm not much help." He gestured toward the bedroom. "I really should check on my mother again."

"One more thing. You were questioned regarding suspicious deaths at another hospital two years before

Mrs. Inman died. Edna Fouts and Lydia Corgin. You worked at Pine Ridge then."

Conrad held up his hand. "Before you go any further, I've been down this road before. Both of those instances were investigated, and it was decided there was no wrongdoing on my part or the hospital's. Besides," he said, emphasizing the word, "in both cases, those were elderly patients who were already critically ill and at high risk when they were admitted."

"But you were asked to leave the hospital," Liam said.

Irritation snapped across the man's beefy face. "The head of the hospital freaked out. So I left on my own. Found a place at Serenity Now. They appreciate me there."

"Yet a patient named Hilda Rogers died on your watch at the nursing facility," Liam said.

"Hilda was ninety-five and developed pneumonia," he said, his tone taking on an edge. "When you work at a nursing facility you lose patients. Look at the statistics, Agent Maverick. Unfortunately, it comes with the job."

"It does. As long as the patients aren't helped along."

Conrad rolled his hands into fists. "I do my job and make the patients comfortable," he said in a gruff voice. "Now. I really need to check on my mother."

He didn't give Liam time to respond. He pushed Liam out the door, then closed it and locked it. Liam gritted his teeth.

The man might be innocent. But he'd planted enough doubt in Liam's mind to warrant further investigation.

PEYTON RACED TOWARD her mother's cottage, her heart in her throat. The attack from her sister yesterday, then another attack last night, and now her mother...

She had to be all right.

Lights from the fire engine twirled against the dark gray skies, and an ambulance was parked in front. The scene was chaotic with some of the residents gathering on the lawn to watch while firefighters raced inside. She threw her car into Park, jumped out and ran toward the cottage. Joanna stood, wringing her hands together and pacing.

"What happened?" she cried as she ran toward Joanna.

"Gas leak," Joanna said. "I smelled it the minute I went in."

Peyton froze, her mind racing. The only gas in the cottage was the fireplace which her mother never turned on. Her hands were too weak.

Which meant someone else had.

The medics were rolling her mother to the ambulance. Joanna hugged her, her eyes wide in fear, making Peyton's stomach clench into a fist-sized knot. Joanna was the calmest, coolest caretaker Peyton had ever met.

If she was worried, her mother's condition was serious.

She wiped at a tear as she ran to the ambulance. Joanna grabbed her arm as if to steady her, and it was a good thing. The sight of her mother unconscious with an oxygen mask over her face stole her breath.

One medic was taking her mother's vitals while the other medic was on his phone calling in to the hospital. Peyton stroked her mother's soft hair from her forehead. "I'm here, Mama. I'm here. Hang in there." But her mother didn't respond.

"We're going to transport her to the hospital," the medic said.

"How is she?" Peyton asked, a note of desperation in her voice.

"Pulse is low and thready. But hopefully we got her out in time."

Peyton gripped the side of the gurney to keep from sinking to the ground. Fear was rapidly taking over, fueled with adrenaline and panic.

She kissed her mother's cheek, then released her hand so the medics could load her onto the ambulance.

While they did, she scanned the lawn and property for her sister or anyone suspicious, but a minute later, the medics said they were ready to leave and shut the back door of the ambulance. She gripped her keys to go to her car, but Joanna caught her arm. "I can drive you, Peyton."

She shook her head. "Stay here and see after my patients," she said. "I'll let you know when I hear something."

Terror knifing through her, she jogged back to her car, started the engine, pulled from the parking lot and followed behind the ambulance.

LIAM SPENT THE next few hours investigating Miller Conrad. He stopped by Jacob's office and set up his laptop in one of the interrogation rooms, then phoned Pine Ridge Hospital.

Anita Arnez, the head nurse for the ER, took his call. He explained that he'd spoken to Conrad. He wanted information on his mother's illness, but he knew damn well that HIPAA would prevent a doctor from divulging personal details. Still, a casual conversation might lead to insight.

"Miller is dependable, punctual, and takes the health-care of his patients seriously."

"Sounds like a glowing recommendation for someone who was asked to leave," Liam said.

She hesitated, then cleared her throat. "Well, yes. The problem was that sometimes he gets a little intense."

"What do you mean?" Liam asked.

"I don't want to slander his reputation," Anita said. "But he and I clashed on how to deal with patients' families. When those two patients died, and questions were being asked, he got defensive and said he'd go work for a place that appreciated him."

"What do you mean about how he deals with families," Liam said, drawing her back on track.

"Well, he reprimanded grown children for not taking better care of their parents. He accused one man of neglecting his mother, and a sister and brother of withholding medication that would make their father more comfortable."

"Were his accusations substantiated?"

"Not that we found, although there definitely are some people who don't treat the elderly well. I don't like it either."

"I imagine he's extra protective because of his mother's illness," Liam murmured.

Another sigh. "You know about her?"

"I stopped by his house and saw her," Liam admitted. "He said she's in the final stages of cancer now."

"Yes, he's certainly devoted to her," Anita said.

So, he was telling the truth about her illness. "Who takes care of her while he's at work?"

A tense heartbeat passed. "I'm sorry, Agent Maverick, but I'm not comfortable discussing Mrs. Conrad's health. You understand."

"Yes, of course." Liam paused, then asked her about the case at Serenity Now. "Were you aware of that?"

"As a matter of fact, the director of Serenity Now phoned and asked me about Conrad after that woman died. But the center found no evidence of wrongdoing."

Just like Whistler Hospital insisted there was no wrongdoing involved in Barry Inman's wife's death.

"I have one more question," Liam said. "You said Mr. Conrad is devoted to his patients and I saw how compassionate he was with his mother. If a patient was terminal with no hope for a cure and in tremendous pain, do you think he might help them to pass?"

A long strained silence stretched between them. "I don't know how to answer that, Agent Maverick. But if I knew of a case where he did that, I would have to report it. Now, excuse me I have to go."

Liam thanked her and ended the call. She didn't know how to answer—but her reaction was an answer in itself.

He checked the file Bennett had sent, then shot him a text asking him to dig deeper into Conrad and the idea he might be a mercy killer.

Bennett texted in return, Copy that. FYI: Conrad's father died while at Golden Gardens.

If he was an angel of mercy, that death could have been his trigger.

PEYTON PACED THE ER while the doctors treated her mother for gas inhalation. They were giving her fluids and oxygen and had connected her to a heart monitor. Her blood pressure and oxygen saturation level were dangerously low, and she hadn't yet regained consciousness.

That worried Peyton the most. Her mother couldn't die.

Guilt niggled at her, and she squeezed her mother's hand. If Val knew her mother might be dying, would she clean up her act and come to the hospital and say goodbye?

Or…would she come and try to steal drugs from her own mother? Was that the reason she'd been at her mother's cottage? Not that they stored narcotics in the residents' homes. The staff monitored the medications.

Residents suffering from memory issues, depression, confusion as a result of illness or aging conditions, and ones too physically challenged to oversee their own medications needed assistance. One could easily overdose if they mixed the wrong meds or overmedicated themselves.

Joanna called for an update, and Peyton choked up. "I don't know if she'll make it. She looks so weak and pale."

"Hang in there, Peyton. I'm praying for her and you."

"Thanks, Jo. I don't know what I'd do without you."

"Try to get some rest. Call me if you need me."

Peyton mumbled she would, hung up, then stepped into the bathroom. She splashed cold water on her face and stared at the bruise on her cheek. Even with makeup, the purple-and-yellow bruising shone through. She traced her fingers over the knot on the back of her head.

He mother's heart monitor suddenly beeped that she was flatlining and Peyton darted from the bathroom. Two nurses and a doctor rushed in.

"Get the crash cart!" the doctor shouted.

"On its way," the nurse responded.

Peyton had assisted in critical situations just like this so many times that it shouldn't phase her. But this was her mother.

She leaned against the wall and watched in silence as the nurse charged the paddles.

Suddenly her phone beeped with a text. One of the nurses shot her an irritated look, and she clenched her phone with a white-knuckled grip as her mother's frail body jerked, then went still again.

Tears blurred in her eyes as she looked down at the text.

YOU WERE WARNED.

Peyton pressed a fist to her mouth to stifle a scream of denial, then watched as the staff desperately worked to save her mother.

Chapter Eleven

Peyton held her breath and sent a prayer to the heavens that her mother would survive.

After two attempts with the paddles, the machine finally beeped indicating a heart rate. Relief whooshed through her, and she sagged against the wall. Perspiration trickled down the back of her neck and her hands felt clammy.

One of the nurses gave her a questioning look. "You okay?"

She nodded although tears burned her eyes, blurring her vision. One nurse pushed the crash cart from the room, while another stayed by her mother's side, checking and adjusting the monitors.

Shock and fear had fueled her adrenaline, but now that that was wearing off, her anger mounted, and the world moved in slow motion.

Suddenly woozy, she muttered she'd be back, then hurried from the room. She stumbled down the hall to the restroom, splashed cold water on her face again and stared at herself in the mirror.

A liar's face stared back. She'd been running scared for five years. If the hospital fire was connected to

Gloria Inman's death, her silence might have caused other people to lose their lives.

Including Agent Maverick's father.

The events of the past played through her head and tears ran freely down her face.

She'd kept silent when questioned about Gloria Inman's death. Lied to the police when they'd asked if she suspected foul play.

Even this week when that agent had shown up, she'd maintained her original story.

But her mother lay in a hospital fighting for her life anyway.

Something had to change. She could not let whoever was doing this dictate her life and hurt her mother.

Her hands trembled as she plucked a paper towel from the holder and wiped her tears away. She refused to be victimized anymore.

She might face consequences for her silence. If she lost her license, how would she support herself and pay for her mother's care?

But if she didn't do something, her mother might die anyway.

Her hand trembled as she retrieved her phone and Agent Maverick's card from her pocket. Another female entered the restroom, and she stepped outside, then walked to the waiting room. Full.

Frustrated and wanting privacy, she headed toward the cafeteria. There, she could blend in with the staff and patients' family members and find a quiet corner to make the call. As she entered, she scanned the room in case someone was watching her.

Although she had no idea who'd sent her that text

message. The voice on the phone from five years ago had been distorted.

Deciding it was too loud in the cafeteria, she headed toward the staff lounge, but since she no longer worked at Whistler Hospital, she didn't have the code to enter. Nerves on edge, she walked back to her mother's room to make certain she was stable. Satisfied when she saw her heart rate had steadied, she told the nurse to call her if there was a problem, that she was going to get coffee.

Then she veered down the hall to an atrium area which housed a coffee shop at one end and small seating alcoves for visitors. She bought a cup of coffee, then claimed an empty table in the corner by the window.

Nerves clawed at her as she pressed Agent Maverick's phone number.

"I'M SORRY, AGENT MAVERICK," Dr. Hammerhead said. "I can't find the toxicology report on Mrs. Inman, although I'm certain I ran one."

"Do you recall seeing anything suspicious?" Liam asked. "A drug interaction?"

"No, but I can't say with all certainty. I've worked on hundreds of autopsies in the past five years. It would be a disservice to simply guess."

Liam's phone buzzed with another call. Peyton Weiss. But he needed to finish this call first. "I'm requesting an exhumation order for Gloria Inman's body. If her death has anything to do with the hospital fire, learning what happened to her is key."

"I'll be happy to work it in when you get approval," Dr. Hammerhead agreed.

"All right. I'll let you know."

Before he returned Peyton's call, he rapped on Jacob's office door. "I want to talk to Inman again."

"New evidence?"

Liam shook his head. "It's about his wife's autopsy."

Jacob retrieved Inman while Liam grabbed the man a bottle of water and carried it to the interrogation room. Inman shuffled in a few minutes later, looking even more ragged than he had when they'd first brought him in. Dark circles rimmed his eyes and despair robbed the color from his face. Liam wondered if he was suicidal as his mother had suggested.

Although he'd had five years to kill himself if he really wanted.

Then again, he was in jail now. Maybe he'd survived because he hadn't had to face the consequences of his actions.

He shuffled through the door, head lowered as Jacob led him to the table. He sat down with a thunk and an angry scowl. "You don't have proof I did anything but leave town after my wife died. And that was after I tried to find out what caused her to die." He muttered a low sound in his throat. "Course I was the only one who wanted the truth."

Liam maintained a neutral expression. "If you're as innocent as you claim, help us prove it."

The man spied the bottle of water, grabbed it, twisted the cap off and gulped down half the bottle. When he set it on the table, he stared directly into Liam's eyes. "What do you want?"

"To exhume your wife's body. Apparently, the toxicology report disappeared. If someone made a mistake in that ER, a new autopsy might prove you were right about the hospital's wrongdoing."

The man's Adam's apple bobbed up and down in his skinny throat as he swallowed. "I thought the lawyers already looked at that."

"True. But the original files were destroyed in the fire. And paperwork can be doctored." If he had the original, he'd have it analyzed for false documentation. Without the original though, it would be impossible to prove it had been tampered with. "I understand exhumation is not a pleasant idea but reexamining her remains could help clear your name. I can proceed without your permission, of course, but having your consent will expedite the process." He leaned forward. "So, if you've nothing to hide, and you want justice, another autopsy would be beneficial."

Inman took another long gulp of water, then set the bottle down. "All right. Then do it."

Inman's cooperation might mean he was telling the truth. Or…if he or Sondra had killed Gloria, they'd used a drug they didn't think could be detected in a tox report.

He made a mental note to ask the ME to search for drugs that weren't typically checked for in a routine autopsy.

Jacob stood. "I'll handle petitioning for the license and approval."

Liam nodded. Hopefully this would bring them one step closer to the truth.

He excused himself, then left the room to see why Peyton had called. Outside in the hall, he checked his messages.

"Agent Maverick, it's Peyton Weiss." Her voice sounded shaky, broken. "I…need to talk to you. Please call me."

Liam's pulse jumped. If Peyton was ready to talk, something must have happened.

He quickly pressed Call Back, then paced the hall. Tense seconds passed before she answered.

"You want to talk?" he asked gruffly. "I'm listening."

Another second passed. She was hesitating. Because she was frightened?

PEYTON TOOK A deep breath. "Not over the phone. Can you meet me?"

"Of course. Your apartment?"

Whoever had sent her that message had been at her place. He might be watching. "No," she said quickly. "Meet me at the Grapevine in River's Edge." It was a funky little wine bar with dim lighting. If she was being watched, it would appear she was on a date, not meeting the agent.

"All right. What time?"

"Half an hour."

She ended the call, then phoned Joanna and asked her to sit with her mother. There was no way she'd leave her alone, not knowing that bastard had almost killed her.

Joanna agreed to come right away, and Peyton hurried to check on her mother. She was resting and stable although still hadn't opened her eyes yet.

"We have a room for her on the second floor and are admitting her," one of the nurses told her. "They'll be moving her soon."

Peyton thanked them, then ducked into the restroom, pulled her compact from her purse and tried to repair her face. Her eyes still looked red and slightly swollen and that bruise made her look downright scary.

For the briefest of seconds, she saw herself as Agent

Maverick must. A scared and emotionally drained woman in trouble.

Fighting humiliation at the thought, she reminded herself that it didn't matter. She didn't care what he thought about her looks, only that he could help her.

She washed away the remnants of her mascara, applied concealer, then dabbed powder over her face and applied a soft pale pink lip gloss. She couldn't show up at the Grapevine looking like she'd been in a bar fight.

The door to her mother's room opened and she peeked from the bathroom door. Joanna poked her head into the room. "Peyton?"

Peyton jammed her compact back into her purse, threw it over her shoulder and stepped into the room. Joanna's worried expression indicated she knew how close Peyton had come to losing her mother.

"I'm sorry to ask—"

"Don't you dare apologize," Joanna said as she pulled Peyton into a hug. "You know you can call me for anything you need. Anytime."

Joanna had been a true friend the past few years, ever since she'd come to Golden Gardens. Her compassion for the senior patients was touching.

"They're admitting her," Peyton explained. "If they move her to a room before I return, stay with her. Okay?"

"Of course. I'll text you the room number."

"Please make sure you verify any medication she's given."

Joanna's brows pinched together. "Is something going on here that I don't know about?"

Peyton shrugged. "I'm probably being paranoid.

I just want to make sure she isn't left alone, not for a minute."

Joanna tugged the collar of her shirt with shaky fingers. "Now you're making me nervous."

"Just promise," Peyton said.

Joanna squeezed Peyton's hand. "I promise."

Peyton gave her a hug, then hurried toward the ER exit. She scanned the waiting room as she passed it in search of someone who might be watching her and checked her surroundings as she dashed toward her car. The temperature had dropped, adding a chill to the air, and she shivered and tugged her jacket around her.

Footsteps sounded behind her just as she wove between a row of cars, and she felt someone behind her. She grabbed her keys and gripped them between her fingers to use as a weapon.

The footsteps grew louder, closing in on her, and a shadow loomed behind her. Fear clawed at her and she fought a scream as she ran for her car.

Chapter Twelve

Peyton stumbled as she reached for the door handle. But she managed to maintain her footing and swung open the door. Footsteps pounded the pavement behind her, and she threw herself into the driver's seat, slammed the door and locked it.

When she looked up, a teenager jogged past and veered toward a Jeep. Relief filled her, and she started the engine, then backed from her parking spot and swerved onto the road. Two more turns and she was headed into the small town of River's Edge.

The quaint little shops and restaurants were lit up, the local inn parking lot filled with tourists who'd come to enjoy the fall colors and local arts and crafts and antiques festival scheduled for the weekend. Others enjoyed the local apple houses where they sold apples and related foods like jams, jellies, apple bread and apple butter.

Several families were out with strollers and kids rode bikes on the sidewalk toward the ice-cream shop. As she parked at the Grapevine, a couple exited their car and strolled arm in arm toward the entrance. They looked so in love that Peyton's heart gave a pang.

Sometimes at night when she was alone, she craved a man's comforting arms. She even imagined a husband and family.

SHE PARKED, PULLED her jacket on, snagged her shoulder bag and glanced around her as she climbed from her car. A shiver rippled through her as she reached the door, and she glanced over her shoulder to see if anyone was following.

Two men in suits walked toward the door along with another couple. She stepped inside, grateful for the dim lighting and soft piano music wafting through the room.

Agent Maverick stood by the hostess station, his dark gaze latching on to her. Her breath caught at how handsome he looked. Instead of his suit, he wore a button-down white shirt and a pair of jeans that accentuated his height and muscles. For a moment, she imagined her life was different, that she was normal like the couple outside. That she was meeting this handsome man for a date.

When in truth, he could arrest her for withholding information in a possible homicide investigation.

He gestured toward the seating area, then the hostess led them to a small round table in the corner. A vineyard scene had been hand painted on the tabletop, and wineglasses waited to be filled. The whole place felt intimate and romantic.

Maybe she should have chosen a coffee shop instead. Her mother's pale face flashed in her mind, and she shook herself back to reality.

"Ms. Weiss?" Agent Maverick said in that deep, commanding voice that reminded her he was a federal agent. "Do you want a drink?"

Did she? "Yes." After today, she needed one.

The waitress appeared and she ordered a Pinot Noir but he ordered coffee. Always on the job. She fidgeted, working up her courage while they waited on the drinks. Needing liquid courage, she took a sip as soon as the wine arrived, but her hand trembled as she set the glass back on the table.

"What's going on?" he asked.

She traced her finger around the stem of her glass. "I have something to tell you. But there's a stipulation."

He raised a dark brow. "I can't promise anything until I hear what you say."

Panic zinged through her, and she stood. "Then this meeting is over."

He caught her arm, his body brushing hers as he stepped up beside her. "Peyton, please sit back down. I can tell you're scared. I want to help you."

Did he? Or would he arrest her if she confessed the truth?

LIAM SENSED PEYTON was ready to bolt even before she stood up. But she'd asked to see him for a reason, and he didn't intend to let her run without divulging what had prompted her call.

"Please, Peyton," he said softly. "Something spooked you. I can see it in your eyes. And I don't think your bruise was just an accident. Tell me what's going on."

Her soft sigh reeked of worry, and indecision played on her face. But she gave a small nod, then sank back into her chair. She sipped her wine again, and he simply waited, allowing her time to put together her thoughts.

"I want protection for my mother," she said in an earnest tone. "That is the deal. Twenty-four-hour around-the-clock protection."

That wasn't what he'd expected to hear. "Your mother is in danger?"

She nodded. "Someone almost killed her today. She's in the hospital now."

Liam narrowed his eyes. "I don't understand. Why would someone want to hurt her?"

"To punish me for talking to you."

She lifted her head and looked into his eyes. God, she was frightened, but she was also so beautiful that his gut clenched.

"But you haven't told me anything."

"I know that, and I did everything he said. But he thinks I talked, and he warned me and now he tried to kill Mama." Her voice cracked and tears blurred her eyes.

Liam inhaled. "You were threatened?"

She nodded again.

He covered her hand with his. Hers felt cold, another sign of nerves. "Why don't you start from the beginning? Who threatened you and why?"

She wiped away a tear. "The truth is, I don't exactly know what happened with Gloria Inman in the ER, and I don't know who set the hospital fire."

"Then what is this about?"

"I have suspicions. But I want to clarify that I wasn't covering for anyone, at least no one that I knew of specifically."

Liam squeezed her hand. "Just tell me what happened in your own words."

She blinked, then sighed again. "Like I said before, Mrs. Inman was in cardiac distress when her husband brought her to the ER. Mr. Inman was distraught. We began to work to save her immediately. Following protocol and Dr. Butler's orders, I gave Gloria a shot of epinephrine to jump-start her heart. We tried CPR, and the paddles, but all our efforts failed."

"But you thought something was wrong?" Liam asked. "Why?"

"I can't put my finger on it," Peyton said. "But Dr. Butler seemed concerned. I saw it in his eyes. When I asked him about it, he acted strange, then he showed me the log report we use to record every medication and form of treatment we use on a patient." She hesitated, her brows furrowed. "That log report showed that I took morphine from the cart and administered it to Gloria Inman." She implored him with her eyes. "But I didn't give her morphine or take morphine from the cart."

Liam frowned. "But the log had your name on it?"

"Each nurse has an individual code for the crash cart which stores all the medications needed in an emergency, at least enough for a first round of treatment. It's part of our system to avoid mistakes or mix-ups. Dr. Butler didn't order morphine. But my security code showed up as the one used to remove it from the cart."

Liam chewed over that information. Butler had lied to him. "What did he say when you told him this?"

"He said the paperwork would prove otherwise, so I should keep quiet about it, that he would investigate and find out if someone had used my code."

"Did he?"

"The next time I asked, he told me that if I didn't want to lose my reputation or my job, I should stay quiet."

"But he never explained about the log?"

She shook her head. "I was going to talk to someone else, go to the hospital administrator, but then I received a threatening message to keep my mouth shut or my mother would end up like Gloria."

Anger knifed through Liam. She could be lying about the threat, although the fear in her eyes was very real. And the wording of that threat suggested that Gloria Inman's death might have been intentional.

"What happened then?"

"A week later, a couple of days after your father questioned me about Gloria Inman's death, the hospital caught fire. I didn't know it was related, but my mother was in the hospital and almost died." She hesitated. "But I got this sick feeling in the pit of my stomach, that the person who threatened me was watching. That he was sending me another warning."

"Do you think Dr. Butler was the person who threatened you?"

She pressed two fingers to her temple. "I honestly don't know. The voice on the phone was disguised. Almost as if it was electronic. I wanted to come forward then, but if I lost my job, I couldn't take care of Mama. So, I moved her to Golden Gardens and took a job there to protect her."

"Have you been threatened during the past five years?"

She winced. "Not until the night you brought me in for questioning. When I got home, someone had broken in. He left a copy of the log from the ER the night Gloria Inman died."

Liam gritted his teeth.

"Then this morning there was a gas leak in Mama's cottage."

"You don't think it was accidental?"

She shook her head. "First of all, Mama never turns on the gas fireplace."

She removed her phone from her purse, then flipped it around to reveal a text. "Then I received this message."

Liam's blood ran cold as he read the text. If everything Peyton said was true and she was being framed, both she and her mother were in danger.

PEYTON HOPED SHE wasn't making a mistake by confiding in the agent. But she'd tried handling the situation on her own, and her mother had almost died anyway.

She needed help.

Agent Maverick cleared his throat. "Uncovering the truth about Gloria Inman's death is the key to keeping you and your mother safe. The autopsy report was destroyed in the hospital fire. I'm having Mrs. Inman's body exhumed and another autopsy performed."

"Does Mr. Inman know?" Peyton asked.

"He does. Which suggests that he doesn't have anything to hide."

"Whoever threatened me is watching me," Peyton said. "He knew you questioned me. He knows where I live and where my mother is."

"I'll arrange for her to have protection twenty-four-seven right away." He covered her hand with his again. "Trust me, Peyton. I'll take care of both of you."

Her breath stalled in her chest. "You're talking about my mother's life, Agent Maverick."

"Call me Liam." Something sparked in his eyes. A hint of concern? Sexual awareness? "I'm putting you in protective custody, as well."

Surprise fluttered through her. "I can't work with a cop following me around."

"I'm not talking about a cop," he said. "I'll protect you myself."

Peyton shivered. The idea of spending more time with the sexy, tough agent unnerved her. It had been a long time since she'd allowed a man to get close to her. And even longer since someone had actually helped her in any way.

"Peyton?" Liam said quietly. "Is there anything else you want to tell me?"

She considered confiding about her sister, but her drug addiction had nothing to do with Gloria Inman's death or the hospital fire. She hoped.

"I was attacked outside my apartment last night."

"Did you see your attacker's face?"

She shook her head. "He hit me from behind and knocked me unconscious. When I came to, he was gone."

"Did your assailant say anything?"

She rubbed her temple again. "No. I opened the sliding glass doors to rescue the resident cat, and a shadow appeared behind me. Before I could turn and look, something struck me in the back of the head."

A muscle ticked in Liam's jaw. "Do you remember anything else? Maybe a smell? How tall he was?"

Peyton searched her memory banks. "It all happened so fast. But…now that you mention it, I did smell something. Like…alcohol. Not booze but rubbing alcohol. Or maybe it was some kind of medicinal soap."

"Like you use at the hospital?"

Peyton nodded.

"So, your attacker could work in the medical field.

And if what you say is true, he was at the hospital the night Gloria Inman died."

Her heart hammered. "And he used my code so if anyone became suspicious, I'd take the fall."

Chapter Thirteen

Liam studied Peyton for signs she was still lying. But she looked so tormented that he had the crazy urge to comfort her. To promise her things he had no business promising.

Not just protection from whoever was threatening her but from the law.

Although technically, she didn't know specific details about the woman's death. But if she'd come forward with her story and her suspicions sooner, the case wouldn't have gone cold.

"Why didn't you call the police when the man attacked you?" he asked.

"I was afraid," she said. "After that first time you interviewed me, I knew I was being watched."

"But you called today."

She ran her finger along the stem of her glass. "Because I did everything he said, and he still hurt my mother." Her voice rose an octave. "You have to understand, Agent Maverick—"

"Liam."

"You have to understand that I wanted to talk, but I was confused about what happened. My mother is all the family I have. And I couldn't risk her life when I didn't know anything specific." Her voice cracked. "I've felt guilty for five years. Every time I saw the news or heard someone talking about the people who lost their lives in the fire, I wondered if Mr. Inman set it or if my silence contributed to the deaths." Tears filled her eyes. "I've had nightmares where I see their faces. Nightmares of losing my mother and having to live with her death on my conscience."

The pain in her voice tore at him, and he squeezed her hand. "You're not alone, Peyton. And you are not going to lose your mother." Not as long as he could help it.

A strained silence stretched between them. She sipped her wine and wiped at a tear trickling down her cheek. But she didn't release his hand. Instead, she tightened her fingers into his palm as if he was her lifeline.

It felt oddly wrong to hold hands with a person he'd considered a suspect. But he couldn't tear his hand away either. Pain, guilt and fear darkened her eyes. The idea of Peyton hurting anyone or intentionally lying to the police to cover for someone seemed unfathomable. Instead, he saw the caring, devoted, loving nurse he'd heard about. A woman who had become a victim.

A woman who only wanted to protect her aging mother.

"Jacob can arrange for one of his deputies to stand guard at your mother's door."

Panic flared in Peyton's eyes. "But then the man who threatened me will know I talked."

"It's the only way, Peyton. He almost killed her anyway. It's time you stood up for the truth and let me and my brother do our jobs."

She shook her head. "I still worry about the threat."

Liam's mind raced. "Okay, how about this? The deputy will be disguised as one of the hospital staff."

Peyton bit down on her lip, but she finally gave a nod and squeezed his hand. "I can live with that. As long as he doesn't get to her, I'll help you any way I can."

"Then you'll let me put a trace on your phone in case this man calls back."

"Absolutely."

Good. The only way she'd be safe was to catch this bastard.

PEYTON'S HAND TREMBLED as she pulled from the parking lot. Liam's warm, masculine hand and soothing voice lulled her into a temporary sense of security.

But she couldn't let down her guard.

Not until they knew what was going on and that the threat to her and her mother was over.

Letting Liam trace her phone calls might help.

Renewed determination filled her.

You have to help me, sis. Someone's after me.

God. What had her sister gotten herself into?

Nerves on edge, she pressed the voice control on her car and asked to call Joanna's number. The phone rang twice, then Joanna finally answered.

"How's Mama?" Peyton said without preamble.

"The same," Joanna said softly as if she didn't want to disturb Peyton's mother. "She hasn't regained consciousness, but she's stable, Peyton."

Fear nearly choked Peyton. "I...can't lose her, Jo."

A heartbeat passed. "I know. She's going to pull through. Your mama's a tough lady."

"4 for 4" MINI-SURVEY

We are prepared to **REWARD** you with 4 FREE Books and Free Gifts for completing our MINI SURVEY!

Suspenseful Romance

Suspense

You'll get up to...
4 FREE BOOKS & FREE GIFTS

FREE
Value Over
$20!

ust for participating in our Mini Survey!

Get Up To 4 Free Books!

Dear Reader,

IT'S A FACT: if you answer 4 quick questions, we'll send you 4 FREE REWARDS from each series you try!

Try **Harlequin® Romantic Suspense** books featuring heart-racing page-turners with unexpected plot twists and irresistible chemistry that will keep you guessing to the very end.

Try **Harlequin Intrigue® Larger-Print** books featuring action-packed stories that will keep you on the edge of your seat. Solve the crime and deliver justice at all costs.

Or **TRY BOTH!**

I'm not kidding you. As a leading publisher of women's fiction, we value your opinions… and your time. That's why we are prepared to reward you handsomely for completing our mini-survey. In fact, we have 4 Free Rewards for you, including 2 free books and 2 free gifts from each series you try!

Thank you for participating in our survey,

Pam Powers

www.ReaderService.com

To get your 4 FREE REWARDS:
Complete the survey below and return the insert today to receive up to 4 FREE BOOKS and FREE GIFTS guaranteed!

"4 for 4" MINI-SURVEY

1 Is reading one of your favorite hobbies?

☐ YES ☐ NO

2 Do you prefer to read instead of watch TV?

☐ YES ☐ NO

3 Do you read newspapers and magazines?

☐ YES ☐ NO

4 Do you enjoy trying new book series with FREE BOOKS?

☐ YES ☐ NO

Please send me my Free Rewards, consisting of **2 Free Books from each series I select** and **Free Mystery Gifts**. I understand that I am under no obligation to buy anything, as explained on the back of this card.

❑ **Harlequin® Romantic Suspense** (240/340 HDL GQ5A)
❑ **Harlequin Intrigue® Larger-Print** (199/399 HDL GQ5A)
❑ **Try Both** (240/340 & 199/399 HDL GQ5M)

FIRST NAME   LAST NAME

ADDRESS

APT.#   CITY

STATE/PROV.   ZIP/POSTAL CODE

EMAIL ❑ Please check this box if you would like to receive newsletters and promotional emails from Harlequin Enterprises ULC and its affiliates. You can unsubscribe anytime.

© 2020 HARLEQUIN ENTERPRISES ULC
® and ™ are trademarks owned and used by the trademark owner and/or its licensee. Printed in the U.S.A.

HI/HRS-520-MS20

But even tough ladies didn't always survive. Her job had taught her that.

"I'm on my way to the hospital. Can you stay until I get there?"

"I promised not to leave her, and I won't. She's in room 310."

Peyton murmured her thanks and hung up. Rain began to drizzle down, fog blurring the road, and she slowed as she rounded a curve. A pair of oncoming headlights nearly blinded her, then the car swerved, tires squealing as it corrected itself into the right lane.

Perspiration dotted her skin, and she maneuvered a bend in the road, then glanced in her rearview mirror to see if Liam was still following her. He was two cars back.

A half mile down the road, a dark SUV pulled out from a side street and barreled toward her. She swerved to avoid being hit but had no place to go as another car was in the oncoming lane. Suddenly the SUV smashed her in the passenger side and sent her into a spin.

She clenched the steering wheel in a white-knuckled grip, brakes squealing. But the force of the impact made her lose control. She hit the guardrail, crashed through it, then her car flipped upside down.

She screamed as she skidded toward the side of the mountain.

LIAM'S HEART HAMMERED as Peyton's car slammed into the rocky mountain wall. The car behind her managed to swing around her and avoid crashing, then drove on while the vehicle that had hit her in the side raced away.

He swerved to the side of the road, and prayed Peyton was all right as his tires screeched and he careened to a stop. As he jumped out and ran toward Peyton's overturned car, he punched Jacob's number. "A car just crashed into Peyton. Dark SUV. Couldn't get the license plate. Send an ambulance." He gave him the address.

"Is Peyton hurt?" Jacob asked.

"I don't know yet. I'm just getting to the car." He ended the call, shoved his phone in his pocket and climbed over the crushed guardrail. His boots skidded on the graveled embankment as he hurried down the hill. When he reached the car, his stomach lurched.

Glass had shattered and sprayed the ground and the front of the car was crunched. Panic shot through him. Peyton could be trapped.

He hurried to the driver's side, stooped down and looked through the broken window. The airbag had deployed, and Peyton was slumped in the seat unconscious.

"Peyton." He called her name over and over as he struggled to open the car door. It was jammed, but finally he managed to yank it open. Then he pulled his pocketknife and slashed at the airbag, ripping it away so he could check her for injuries.

He pressed two fingers to her neck to feel for a pulse. Seconds ticked by. "Peyton, wake up."

Finally, he felt a pulse, then she groaned and opened her eyes.

"What happened?" she asked on a ragged breath.

"You had an accident. Don't move. Medics are on the way." He stroked her hair from her forehead and noticed blood at her temple. "Are you hurt?"

"I...don't know," she mumbled.

"Can you move your arms?"

She slowly lifted one hand, then the other, then coughed. "My chest hurts."

"The airbag," Liam said. "You probably bruised or cracked a rib or two. How about your legs?"

Her face pinched into a frown as she struggled to move. "My legs are trapped." Panic tinged her tone.

Dammit. He brushed her cheek with his thumb. "Just stay still. Medics are on the way," he repeated.

Terror filled her eyes. "Mama…"

"Jacob sent a deputy to the hospital," Liam assured her.

She closed her eyes with a groan, and fear clawed at him. The SUV that had hit her came out of nowhere. It hadn't slowed or even attempted to stop after the crash.

His gut clenched. Had the crash been intentional? An attack on Peyton?

A siren wailed, and lights twirled in the sky as a fire engine and Jacob's squad car roared up. They careened to a stop behind his vehicle, then Jacob and the firefighters jumped out and raced down the embankment.

"She's alive, but her legs are trapped!" he shouted. One of the firefighters raced back to the truck for equipment, and Jacob and the medic approached.

"I didn't attempt to move her," Liam said, knowing he could have caused worse damage if he had. She needed to be boarded and her neck secure before pulling her from the car. "She has a pulse and regained consciousness long enough to move her arms. Don't know how badly her legs are injured. She complained of a sore chest."

The firefighter hurried toward them, and Liam stood back and watched as they used the Jaws of Life to cut

Peyton out of the car. She groaned and stirred again, and Liam squeezed her hand.

"The medics are taking you to the hospital," he said. "You're going to be okay, Peyton."

Yet a helpless feeling overcame him as he watched the medics secure her neck and ease her onto the board.

"Liam?" she called.

"I'm here," he assured her. "I'll follow the ambulance."

She sighed, then closed her eyes again, then the medics loaded her onto the ambulance and closed the door.

Liam turned to Jacob. "Get a forensics team to process her car. Tell them to look for paint samples from the SUV that hit her."

"You think it was an accident?"

Liam shook his head. "No. I think the person threatening Peyton just tried to kill her."

PEYTON DRIFTED IN and out of consciousness as the ambulance rocked back and forth. The shrill sound of the siren was giving her a headache.

But she thanked God that her legs hadn't been broken or worse...that she could move them. When she'd realized the front of the car had crunched in on her, she was terrified of being paralyzed.

Then what good would she be to her mother or the other patients who needed her?

Her life flashed in front of her eyes. No more nursing. No family or baby of her own.

Odd, but she hadn't considered finding love or her own family the past few years. Taking care of her mother and the guilt weighing on her had consumed her time and her thoughts. But when the car had spun out of control and slammed into the rocky wall, she'd realized she wanted all those things.

Liam's handsome face taunted her. If things were different, she'd be attracted to the sexy agent. Heck, she *was* attracted to him. What red-blooded woman wouldn't be?

But he saw her as a suspect. Had interrogated her. And he still might arrest her and send her to jail.

The ambulance veered to the right, then slowed and she realized they were stopping.

"We're here." The medic introduced herself as Helen.

They opened the back door, and carefully hauled her out, then rushed her into the ER. As a nurse, she knew the drill, although she hated being a patient.

They wheeled her into a room, began checking vitals and the attending ER doc on duty and a resident examined her. The next two hours were filled with tests, blood work and endless questions.

Liam stood by the room as if on guard, his dark eyes assessing as he watched the hospital staff at work. She'd asked him to inform Joanna of what was going on, and Jacob's deputy watched her mother while Joanna rushed down to see her.

Peyton's friend gave her a hug. "My God, Peyton, are you okay?"

"Nothing broken, thank God," she murmured. Although how could she be okay when someone had tried to kill her and her mother?

"That agent said it was a hit-and-run. The driver didn't even stop to see if you were okay?"

She shook her head. He hadn't stopped because he'd thought she was dead.

When he learned she'd survived, would he come back to finish her off?

Chapter Fourteen

While Peyton's friend Joanna visited her, Liam conferred with Jacob and his deputy Martin Rowan outside Mrs. Weiss's room. Another deputy had arrived at the scene of the crash and stayed to supervise the evidence-recovery team while they processed the scene and had Peyton's car towed to the lab for forensics analysis.

"I want a limited staff taking care of Mrs. Weiss," Liam said. "And those employees vetted."

"I'll handle that," Jacob offered. "FYI, coordinating the timing for the exhumation. I'll let you know when it's done and she's at the morgue."

"So, who or what am I looking for here?" Deputy Rowan asked.

"I wish I had a name or a face," Liam answered. "Peyton said the caller's voice sounded male." He pulled a photo of Dr. Butler from his phone. "This is the doc who was on duty the night Gloria Inman died. He's still at Whistler Hospital, so if he shows up here, don't let him in the room with Mrs. Weiss."

"You think the doctor tried to kill Peyton?" Jacob asked.

"I don't know, but he's a person of interest." He accessed a photo of Herbert Brantley, and then one of

Miller Conrad. "Both of these men are also suspects. Call me if they show up, and don't let him near Mrs. Weiss either."

Deputy Rowan nodded in understanding.

"Peyton's friend Joanna has been with Peyton's mother. Consult with her if Mrs. Weiss is given any medication. We want to make sure someone doesn't sneak in and try to kill her while she's too weak to know what's happening."

"No one will hurt her while I'm on guard," Deputy Rowan assured him.

"I'm going to send a forensics team to Golden Gardens," Jacob said. "And I'll follow up about the paint sample from that vehicle that hit Peyton."

Liam checked his phone for messages from Bennett. He still wanted more info on Herbert Brantley and Miller Conrad. But Bennett hadn't responded yet. The men dispersed, and Liam headed back to Peyton's room.

When he reached the door, she was trying to get out of bed. "I've been examined. I'm fine."

Joanna gripped Peyton's arm. "You're not going anywhere tonight, Peyton. The doctor wants you to rest."

"I don't need to rest," Peyton insisted. "I need to be with Mama."

"You look a mess," Joanna said. "Is that the way you want her to see you when she wakes up? You'll scare her to death."

Peyton went still, then sank back onto the bed with a frustrated sigh. "I just don't want her to be alone. If she wakes up and I'm not there, she'll know something is wrong."

Joanna sank onto the bed beside Peyton and put her arm around Peyton's shoulder. "I promise I'll stay with her tonight. And if she wakes up, I'll come and get you. Okay?"

"You have to be exhausted," Peyton said.

"We both know how to handle long shifts," Joanna said with a small smile. "So, don't worry about me. I'll be in your mother's room so you can rest, and tomorrow I'll bring you to see her. Deal?"

Peyton nodded, although she looked miserable. Joanna gave her a hug and stood. "Call me if you need anything. I'm right upstairs."

"I will. Thanks, Jo."

As Joanna left the room, turmoil suffused Peyton's face. He crossed the room to her and claimed the chair beside her bed. "Deputy Rowan is guarding your mother. He has strict instructions not to let anyone but the staff into the room. With Joanna there, she'll be safe for the night."

Peyton muttered okay, although she didn't sound convinced. He understood her distrust and fear and hated she'd been put in this position when she'd dedicated her life to helping others.

He placed his hand over hers, determined she know she wasn't alone. "Joanna is right. You won't be any good to your mother if you don't take care of yourself."

She winced as she tugged the covers over herself, a reminder she'd bruised her ribs. Then a tear rolled down her cheek as she closed her eyes. Liam gently wiped away the tear and settled into the chair.

Gloria Inman had died in a hospital. One of the medical staff might have been responsible. Not knowing exactly who was to blame made it even scarier for her to be alone.

Someone could disguise themselves as a staff member, sneak in and try to kill her.

Sweat broke out on his brow. He wouldn't leave her side all night.

PEYTON WRESTLED WITH SLEEP through the night. First the nightmares of the crash. *She was flying toward the mountain, skidding and slamming into it. Her own scream echoed in her ears.*

Then the ghostly faces of all the people who'd died in the fire.

It's your fault. You could have saved us.

Val: You have to help me, sis. Someone's after me.

Her mother's cries filled the air. I won't be around forever. Take care of Val.

But she'd tried and failed. And now her mother was dying.

Then she was running, tripping, falling into the darkness as she darted through the woods. A shadowy figure chased her, clawing at her, his footsteps crunching dry, dead leaves as he closed in on her. She panted for a breath, forced one foot in front of the other, climbed the hill, wove among the thick mass of trees. She increased her pace, pushing weeds and tree limbs aside. A sharp branch slapped her in the face. Her foot caught on a tree root. She stumbled, grappling for control and lost the battle.

Then she careened forward over the edge of the ridge. The drop-off was a half mile long. She clawed at the ground, at tree branches and brush, but they slipped through her fingers and she went plunging over the ridge.

She screamed and jerked awake, fighting the air as

if she was still falling. But two strong hands caught her just before she smashed into the rocky canyon below.

"Shh, you're safe now, Peyton."

A man's voice. Gruff. Tender. Concerned.

She blinked and looked up into Liam's eyes. The sexy federal agent who'd asked her to trust him. He rubbed slow circles over her back.

"You had a nightmare," he said in a low voice. "It's over now and you're safe."

She leaned into him, trembling and shaken. Was she safe? If the man who'd tried to kill her worked in the medical field, he could slip in and she'd never know she was in danger.

"I'm not going to let anything happen to you," Liam said quietly. "Go back to sleep, Peyton."

She sighed and laid back against the pillow again, missing his arms when he released her.

GRATEFUL PEYTON FINALLY seemed to rest, Liam pulled the recliner next to her. If anyone attempted to get near Peyton, they'd have to walk past him and around the foot of the bed.

Not going to happen.

He'd taught himself long ago how to catnap in short stretches and remain in tune to any sound when he was on a stakeout or working a case.

Tonight no one would bother Peyton.

He closed his eyes, frustrated that the case had him stumped. He felt like someone had dropped a puzzle on the floor and the pieces had scattered in a hundred directions. He couldn't quite make them fit back together.

Mentally he reviewed the facts he knew to date, then

pulled out a notepad from his pocket and jotted down his thoughts.

His first question—had someone in the hospital made a mistake that cost Gloria Inman her life? Or had she been murdered?

The fact that Dr. Butler, the attending physician, had encouraged Peyton to keep silent regarding the possibility of negligence suggested a mistake had been made. The threat she received also added credence to a hospital cover-up or foul play.

But who was responsible? Peyton? Dr. Butler? Another staff member?

According to Peyton, Dr. Butler had evidence proving her code had been used to remove morphine from the medicine cart. What if Dr. Butler had made the mistake in the ER, then faked the incriminating paperwork against Peyton to save his own reputation?

Mrs. Inman's tox report was missing. And the files for the night she'd died had been destroyed in the fire. All suspicious.

The only two people with motive for killing Gloria were her husband and Sondra Evans, and both claimed they were innocent. However, both had access to drugs via their jobs as pharmaceutical reps.

Liam ran his fingers through his hair.

Peyton still hadn't given him a complete list of everyone who'd been in the ER that night. When she woke up, he'd press her to write down the names.

Logic led them to believe that the fire had been set to cover up whatever had happened that night. That Dr. Butler wanted to save his own reputation by passing the blame on to Peyton.

Frustration tightened his chest. Although that was

the most logical conclusion, he had to remain open to other possibilities.

Herbert Brantley's financials had improved drastically after Mrs. Inman's death. As a med tech, his salary was modest. If he'd witnessed foul play the night Gloria died, he could have been paid to keep silent—or to set the fire and destroy evidence.

Then there was Miller Conrad, the PA who had a soft spot for seniors. He'd been questioned regarding deaths at other medical facilities. He could be an angel of mercy.

Although Gloria Inman hadn't been elderly or on her deathbed.

He rubbed a hand over his bleary eyes and leaned his head back with a sigh. Hopefully tomorrow the exhumation would take place, and the ME could analyze Mrs. Inman's remains. Forensics might give them a solid lead.

Next, he'd question Dr. Butler and Herbert Brantley. One way or the other, he intended to make them talk.

PEYTON WOKE TO the soft sound of someone breathing. Confused, she blinked to clear her vision and realized she was in the hospital. The past twenty-four hours returned in a rush, and she jerked to a sitting position.

The man next to her bed startled and opened his eyes. Then she realized his hand had been lying over hers. She'd felt it during the night when she was in the throes of her nightmares.

Had sensed his comforting presence and had been able to drift back to sleep because she knew he was by her side.

It's only temporary. Don't get used to it.

As soon as they solved this case, he'd disappear from her life.

"Peyton?" Liam asked. "Another nightmare?"

"Just reality," she said softly.

He shifted and ran his fingers through his hair. He looked rumpled and sexy and so masculine that a tingle went through her. He represented everything that was good about a man. Strength and honor. After living in fear for five years, he was just what she needed.

She pushed at the covers to get up. "I need to check on Mama."

He held up a finger. "Wait. I'll text Deputy Rowan."

"I want to see her myself." She shoved the covers away, then realized she was wearing a hospital gown and nothing else. "Where are my clothes?"

"I'll ask the nurse." He stood and looked down at her, the dark flecks in his eyes flaring with concern. "How do you feel?"

She shifted and pressed a hand to her chest as she breathed. "A little sore, but I'm okay." She glanced around the room. "Check that closet. Maybe the nurse put my clothes in there."

He gave a little nod, crossed the room and found a plastic hospital bag in the closet. He retrieved it and brought the bag to her.

"While I change, please ask the nurse to get my release papers."

He arched a brow. "Are you sure you're ready for that?"

No, but she didn't like being a patient. And if her sister returned to her apartment—or if the man who'd threatened her did—she wanted to be there.

Liam stepped from the room, and she dressed

quickly. Bruises darkened her chest and arms and legs. She was sore all over, but nothing was broken. All in all, she'd come out of that crash better than she'd expected.

She was alive. So was her mother. That was all that mattered.

By the time Liam returned with the nurse, she was dressed and ready to leave.

"Let's check your vitals one more time," the nurse said. "The doctor wants to make sure they're stable before he releases you."

Peyton choked back a protest. She knew the drill, but impatience nagged at her. Knowing what it was like to deal with difficult patients, she allowed the nurse to do her job. The doctor came in a few minutes later and examined her.

"Do you feel nauseated? Any dizziness?"

She shook her head. "I know the symptoms of a concussion and what to do. But I'm fine. Really."

He signed off on her release and the nurse hurried to retrieve a wheelchair. Liam stood silently by, watching quietly. When the nurse entered with the chair, Peyton told her she wanted to go see her mother, and the nurse pushed her to the elevator. Again, Liam stood by, quiet and protective. When they reached her mother's room, he spoke with the deputy who was dressed in scrubs as a disguise.

Joanna was asleep in the recliner, so Peyton dismissed the nurse, then crossed the room to her mother's bed. Joanna stirred from sleep and looked up at her just as Peyton pressed her hand over her mother's.

Her hand felt warm, a good sign. And her breathing seemed steadier.

"They took her off the oxygen and she's breathing on her own," Joanna said.

Another good sign. Except that her mother still hadn't woken up. "I don't understand why she hasn't regained consciousness," she murmured.

"Her body obviously needs rest," Joanna reminded her. "You know age makes it more difficult to recover. But she'll come through this."

Peyton didn't like to be reminded of her mother's age. No matter what she did, one day her mother would leave this world.

Pain squeezed at her heart. Then she would be all alone.

And that thought terrified her.

Chapter Fifteen

"Any problems last night?" Liam asked Deputy Rowan.

The deputy shook his head no. "Mrs. Weiss rested all night. Joanna stayed in the room with her and talked to the nurses when they checked her vitals." He glanced at his watch. "Sheriff Maverick is sending over my replacement soon."

"Thanks," Liam said. "Go home and get some rest yourself. Hopefully this protective detail won't last long, but until we figure out who tried to kill Mrs. Weiss, we can't leave her without protection."

Liam poked his head in and asked Peyton and Joanna if they wanted coffee. Joanna stood and stretched. "I'm going home to shower and get to work."

"I'd like coffee," Peyton said softly.

"I'll be right back."

Liam took the elevator to the lower floor. A flurry of noise came from the ER as the doors whooshed open and two medics rushed in pushing a gurney. Miller Conrad raced beside them, his breath panting out.

Liam veered into the waiting area just as the medics started to push Conrad's mother through the double doors. "What happened?"

"She's having trouble breathing. I didn't want her to

die at home." Anguish tinged his tone. "I have to go." Conrad raced behind his mother and the medics through the double doors.

Liam headed to the cafeteria, picked up a couple of muffins and coffee, then texted Bennett. Update on Miller Conrad and Herbert Brantley?

Bennett responded, Working on it.

He sent Jacob a text, too. Exhumation?

Jacob: Ten o'clock this morning. Will keep you posted.

Antsy, Liam strode back to the elevator and hurried upstairs to check on Peyton. When he arrived at her mother's room, the deputies were trading shifts. Peyton sat by her mother's bed, her head bowed.

His heart ached for her. She looked so lost, alone and terrified that he wanted to make things right for her.

Deputy Rowan briefed the other deputy, then Liam showed him a photo of Herbert Brantley, then one of Miller Conrad. "If one of these men shows up, call me immediately. And do not, for any reason, allow them to enter Mrs. Weiss's room."

He didn't like the fact that Conrad was downstairs, in the same hospital as Peyton's mother. He didn't like it one damn bit.

PEYTON DIDN'T WANT to leave her mother, but the doctor assured her that she was stable. After she'd finished the coffee and muffin, she'd looked at her reflection in the bathroom mirror. Not wanting to frighten her mother when she woke up, she needed to shower and camouflage her bruises.

Besides, she was so stiff and sore she could barely

move without groaning. And she refused to be a weakling in front of the agent.

The sight of Liam talking to the deputy gave her a small measure of relief. With her mother under protective custody, she had to do everything in her power to help Liam find the person who'd hurt her.

She kissed her mother's cheek. "Rest up, Mama. When you're better, our life will be good again." Hopefully, she could stop looking over her shoulder and living in fear.

She made the deputy promise not to leave her mother's room, and he assured her he would watch over her as if she was his own mother. Liam placed his hand at the small of her back and walked her to the elevator. Peyton gritted her teeth to keep from wincing with every step she took.

"Are you sure you don't need to stay in the hospital for observation for another day?"

"I'm sure." She tugged her jacket around her as they exited the elevator. Before they passed the ER, Liam stopped and pulled her into the waiting room.

"What's wrong?" she asked.

"Do you remember a male PA named Miller Conrad? He worked at Whistler at the same time you did." Liam removed his phone and showed her the man's photograph.

Peyton's heart stuttered. The man definitely looked familiar.

"He was working the night Gloria Inman died," Liam explained.

She massaged her temple in thought. "I think he was there, but not in the room with Gloria." If she had the hospital records, she'd know for sure. But the fire complicated everything.

"Why are you asking about him?" Peyton questioned.

Liam spoke in a whisper. "According to people he worked with, he has a soft spot for seniors. And he's intensely critical of family members who he perceives aren't taking care of their parents."

Peyton narrowed her eyes. "I don't understand. Where are you going with this?"

"Three patients died suspicious deaths at medical facilities where he worked. Did you know that?"

Peyton's pulse jumped. "No."

"His father was also a resident of Golden Gardens and died there."

Cold fear washed over Peyton. "But he's not employed at the Gardens."

"No. But as a visitor, he probably learned his way in and out of the place, and how to avoid security."

He was right. "I asked our security guard to pull the tapes around Mama's the night that man broke in my place. Mama said she saw a man earlier."

"Then she might be able to identify him," Liam said.

"Oh, God," Peyton whispered. "That's why he tried to kill her."

Footsteps sounded, then she saw Miller Conrad emerge through the double doors leading from the ER exam rooms to the waiting room.

"His mother is terminal," Liam said. "He just brought her in."

Judging from the way his shoulders were slumped, the news wasn't good.

The man looked up and saw her and Liam, and his body tensed.

Liam crossed to him. "How's your mother?"

Conrad shook his head. "She's gone." He pinched the bridge of his nose and rushed outside.

Liam motioned for Peyton to follow him to the nurse's desk where he identified himself and asked to speak to the attending physician. A minute later, a tall woman in a white coat appeared and introduced herself.

Liam quickly explained that Miller Conrad was a person of interest in a possible homicide and that he wanted an autopsy performed on Conrad's mother. "The formal request will be on your desk in an hour."

She simply nodded, then disappeared back into the ER.

Peyton clutched Liam's arm. "If you think he's the man who threatened me and hurt my mother, he might come back here."

Liam rubbed her back. "It's possible, but he's distraught, and he knows I'm here. He'd be stupid to try something else right now." He offered her an encouraging look. "Besides, I showed the deputy Conrad's photograph and gave him orders to call me if he shows up, and not to let him in to see your mother."

Peyton's pulse pounded. "I still don't like leaving her."

"She's safe now. Let's go look at that security footage. If Conrad is on them, I'll have enough to bring him in for questioning."

QUESTIONS STILL RATTLED around inside Liam's brain. Conrad's sympathy for seniors and his turmoil over his mother's condition could trigger him to commit mercy killings or even assisted suicide. But he didn't see the connection between him and Gloria Inman.

Mrs. Inman had been late forties and had years of life ahead.

Although…the possibility of assisted suicide led to another point. What if Conrad was paid by the people to help end their lives? Either by the elderly patient or one of their family members who no longer wanted to see them suffer?

His phone dinged with a call.

Peyton twisted her hands together as he drove toward Golden Gardens, and he pressed Bennett's number. "I'm driving. You're on Speaker. Peyton Weiss is with me, but you can speak freely. What do you have?"

"It's about the two patients who died at the hospital where Conrad worked. First Edna Fouts, seventy-nine. Suffered from Parkinson's complicated by delusions and memory loss associated with the disease. She was in stage five, had fallen several times, was unable to get out of bed, and experienced deep vein thrombosis. She died in her sleep."

"Was an autopsy performed?"

"No, the family said she'd suffered enough. They didn't want to put her through anything else."

Dammit. "Go on."

"Patient number two—Lydia Corgin, eighty-three. Suffered from Alzheimer's. Again, late stages. She'd stopped getting out of bed, refused to eat and drink. Then she developed pneumonia. Again, no autopsy."

Liam's chest tightened. "And the third?"

"Conrad took the job at Serenity Now after that. Hilda Rogers, eighty-one, had a history of heart failure. She suffered a stroke and died in her room before the ambulance arrived. Again, no autopsy. Doctor and family agreed that she was ready to go. Son stated that he was glad she was finally at peace."

Liam bit back a curse. "Listen, Bennett, it's possible these deaths were natural causes. But we can't discount mercy killings. In light of the fact that none of them were autopsied, we also could be dealing with assisted suicides."

"I'll research his financials and see if there's anything off," Bennett said. "And I'll start looking at the families. See if there's anything strange about their insurance policies or financials."

Peyton was watching him, anxiety radiating from her rigid posture, as he ended the call.

"I understand why you suspect Conrad of killing those other women, but why would he hurt Gloria Inman? She had health issues, but she wasn't terminal."

"Maybe not. But what if Inman wanted out of his marriage and he learned Conrad could be paid to help. Maybe he took advantage of that. Or he could have even blackmailed Conrad into killing Gloria."

Peyton paled, and Liam pressed Jacob's number to fill him in on his latest theory.

He could be wrong. The pieces were still floating around in his head and he hadn't yet connected them. They might not all be related either.

But at this point, he couldn't discount any possibility.

PEYTON COULDN'T SHAKE her worry for her mother as Liam parked in front of the main building at Golden Gardens. Was Miller Conrad a mercy killer or a killer for hire?

She texted Fred that they'd arrived, and he met them

at the front door and led them to his office. "I already pulled the footage," Fred said.

"Did you look at it?" Peyton asked.

"I haven't had a chance," he said. "It's been a crazy day."

"What do you mean?" Peyton asked.

The age lines around Fred's mouth thinned with his frown. "We lost a patient," Fred said quietly. "Leon."

The hair on the back of Peyton's neck bristled. Leon Brittles who'd seen Val the other night.

"What happened?" Peyton asked.

"I don't know exactly. You'll have to ask Dr. Sweetwater. She rushed to try to save him, but it was too late. His body is on its way to the funeral home."

Liam's suspicions about a mercy killer or assisted suicide taunted her.

Poor Leon. He had no family. No one to call. No one to ask questions about his death.

Chapter Sixteen

Peyton inhaled a deep breath. "How did Leon die?"

Fred pulled a hand down his chin. "All I know is that he wandered out in the garden sometime during the night. Ms. Marley found him this morning when she went for a walk after breakfast. She was pretty upset. Dr. Sweetwater gave her a sedative to calm her down."

Poor lady.

Liam cleared his throat. "Was Leon seriously ill?"

"He had Alzheimer's, and got confused a lot," Peyton said. "But he was mobile and wasn't suffering from any other fatal disease."

Liam folded his arms. "Did Dr. Sweetwater order an autopsy?"

Fred shrugged. "I have no idea."

"I'll call her and ask." Peyton pulled her phone from her purse and pressed the geriatrician's number. She answered on the third ring. "I heard about Leon," Peyton said. "Did you order an autopsy?"

"No," she replied. "I didn't see a need at his age."

"I'm here with Special Agent Liam Maverick," Peyton said.

Liam gestured for her to let him have the phone, and

she handed it to him. He stepped aside, and she heard him request an autopsy.

"Did Ms. Marley say she saw anything suspicious when she found Leon?" Peyton asked Fred.

Fred twirled a toothpick in the corner of his mouth. "Not that I know of. Just that he was lying in the rose-bushes when she got there."

Peyton wanted to talk to Ms. Marley herself. "About those tapes I asked for?"

"I made you a copy." He pulled an envelope from his desk and handed it to her.

"Agent Maverick will want footage of the rose garden last night and this morning. Can you pull that?"

"Give me a few minutes." Fred ran a hand through his thinning hair. "What's going on, Peyton? First you tell me someone broke into your place, now you're acting like there might be foul play surrounding Leon's death."

"I don't know exactly," Peyton said. "But Agent Maverick is thorough." She showed him a picture of Miller Conrad. "Have you seen this man around here?"

Fred adjusted his glasses and peered at the photograph. "That's Miller. His daddy was here. Died in his room."

"Have you seen him at the Gardens lately?"

"Sure have. He got real friendly with some of the residents when he visited his daddy. Every now and then he drops by, so they know he still cares."

Peyton's breath caught. "Did he visit Leon?"

"Sometimes. They liked to play pinochle together."

But Leon wasn't critically ill so a mercy killing wouldn't fit. And he had no family who might want to cash in on his finances when he died.

Unless he'd seen something, like the man who'd broken into her place. But even if he had witnessed something, he would make an unreliable witness.

A shudder coursed up her spine. *He saw Val.*

Val had been at the hospital the night Gloria Inman died, too. And the night of the fire.

She shook her head at the thought of her sister hurting Leon or anyone else. Val was a drug addict, had been caught stealing to pay her dealer and feed her habit. But Val wouldn't hurt anyone.

Would she?

LIAM WAS SURPRISED the geriatrician hadn't ordered an autopsy. Granted the residents in the Gardens were older and had health issues, but stories of abuse to the elderly, especially in nursing-care facilities, abounded.

Relatives and friends had to be vigilant about checking on their loved ones.

Although Peyton kept a close eye on her mother and her care, people like Leon had no one to make sure they weren't being mistreated.

"Dr. Sweetwater, have you noticed unusual bruises or injuries on any of the residents?"

"Nothing that seemed suspicious," Dr. Sweetwater answered.

"How about complaints about the staff?"

"Agent Maverick, I hate to say this but many of the people have health and memory issues that affect their behavior and thoughts, so yes, they complain. Sometimes dementia changes a person's personality. They may be agreeable one minute and belligerent the next. Others suffer from delusions and paranoia resulting from their health issues or medication." She paused. "I hear everything—complaints about how bad the food is, that the cook is trying to poison them, that someone came into their room and stole things, that one of the other residents is trying to kill them. I have to sort it out for the truth, but I can assure you, if I suspected someone was hurting one of my patients, I would report it." She exhaled. "Now, why are you asking these questions? Do you think Leon Brittles's death was suspicious?"

"I'm not at liberty to say at the moment, but if you see or hear anything that raises a red flag, please give me a call."

She agreed, and he returned to Peyton. She handed him a brown envelope. "Tapes from the night of the break-in. I also had Fred pull ones of the garden last night and this morning."

"Good work." He thanked Fred, then drove Peyton to her apartment. She was moving slowly, and he'd noticed her wince when she breathed, a sign she'd suffered more in the car crash than she wanted to admit.

"Thanks for driving me back," she said. "While you were on the phone and Fred was pulling the other tapes, I called my insurance company about my car. I'll probably have to get a rental until we settle, and I can buy a new one."

"Don't worry about it for now," Liam told her. "I'll be driving you around until the threat to you is over."

Fear and another emotion he didn't quite recognize flickered in her eyes.

"Do you want to look at those tapes now?" she asked.

His phone buzzed with a text. Jacob. "Go get a shower first," he said, knowing it would make her feel better. "I'll check in with Jacob."

"Okay, but I want to look at them with you. I might be able to help."

"Good. You can tell me if anyone looks out of place."

She dropped her purse onto the table by the door, while Liam searched and cleared the house, then she rushed into the hall and disappeared into her bedroom.

Liam crossed to the sliding glass doors and looked outside while he phoned Jacob. He explained about the man's sudden death at Golden Gardens and the fact that he'd requested an autopsy.

"You suspect Mr. Brittles's death is related to the threat against Peyton and her mother?" Jacob asked.

"I don't know, but something's going on, and I'm going to get to the bottom of it." He explained about seeing Miller Conrad at the hospital and his mother's death.

"She's going to be autopsied, too?" Jacob asked.

"At my request." Liam swallowed. "I have security tapes from Golden Gardens to review," he told Jacob. "If there was foul play, maybe it was caught on camera."

"Let me know what you find," Jacob said. "FYI, I have more on Herbert Brantley. He had a motorcycle wreck four years ago and suffered some serious injuries. HIPAA laws prevented me from obtaining his full medical history, but I did some digging around. Asked a couple of his neighbors. One of them says Herbert has a drug problem. Pills. He caught him stealing some of his daughter's ADHD medication from his medicine cabinet."

"Did he press charges?"

"No," Jacob said. "Herbert begged him not to and promised to get help."

"Did he?"

"There's no record to prove it one way or the other," Jacob said. "But again, getting medical records these days is not easy." Jacob paused. "Anyway, knowing he stole drugs is enough to warrant bringing him in for questioning."

Liam scrubbed a hand over his face as he tried to maneuver the pieces into a whole picture again. "So, if Herbert had a drug problem, he might have been desperate for money to feed his habit. That could mean he'd accepted money to kill Gloria Inman. But what about the three other patients, Edna Fouts, Lydia Corgin and Hilda Rogers? Does he have a connection to any of them and the facilities where they died?"

"He worked at Whistler Hospital," Jacob said. "He wasn't an employee at the other medical facilities, but with his training and the right clothing, he could easily have slipped in to a patient's room unnoticed."

True. "I'm aware we have limited hospital footage from the night of the fire, and Mrs. Inman's death, but look through them again and see if he was there. And push the ME to rush her autopsy. If someone is killing seniors, we need to hurry."

"Copy that."

What that had to do with Gloria Inman or the fire, he didn't know. "I'll get back to you after I review the footage at Golden Gardens."

He hung up, then set his laptop on the kitchen table and booted it up, anxious to see if Miller Conrad or Herbert Brantley showed up in the tapes.

Peyton had looked so vulnerable earlier. The only way to protect her was to uncover the truth.

No matter what it took.

THE WARM WATER felt heavenly on Peyton's aching body and helped massage the tension from her shoulders.

She scrubbed her skin and soaped her hair, desperate to wash away the dried blood from her forehead and the perspiration permeating her skin.

Although no amount of scrubbing could eliminate the fear seizing her chest. A chest bruised from an intentional car crash meant to take her life.

The water started to cool, and she turned off the spray, climbed out, dried off and wrapped her hair in a towel. She pulled on a clean pair of jeans and her favorite blue sweater, one that accentuated her eyes. Not that it mattered.

Liam had seen her at her worst. And he certainly wasn't interested in her romantically.

If only things were different…

Sighing in frustration, she blew her hair dry, then brushed the waves over her shoulder and headed toward the door from her bedroom to the hall. Although the hair on her nape bristled again.

Instantly tense, she paused in the doorway and scanned the room. The jewelry stand on her dresser was in place. Her bed was made up, although the three decorative pillows she kept on top were thrown haphazardly on the bed. Not how she'd left them.

Someone had been in her room.

She visually swept it for a sign as to whom, looking for a threatening message or another warning. Then she spotted a folded piece of paper on her desk in the corner.

A paper folded into an origami swan.

Her breath caught. When she and Val were little, they loved origami. They left secret messages for each other all over the house and the yard in the intricately folded shapes. Her fingers trembled as she unfolded the swan, then her heart stuttered at the sight of her sister's shaky handwriting.

They're going to kill me, sis. Look below the bench in the rose garden.

Peyton went cold inside. The rose garden was where they'd found Leon's body.

LIAM WAS WORRIED about Peyton. She'd been through a lot lately, both physically and emotionally.

He'd been a wreck when they'd hauled his father from the fire, and he'd lain there limp and pale. When the medics' attempts to save him had failed, he'd literally been driven to his knees. The feelings of helplessness, anger and grief had overwhelmed him that night and for months afterward.

His only saving grace had been his intense need to find the person responsible.

Though he hadn't quite figured it out, the sense that he was closing in on the truth fueled him with adrenaline. He refused to give up.

Even if he had to pressure Peyton.

Still, concern for her knotted his gut. She didn't deserve to live in fear.

He strode to her bedroom door and knocked. "Peyton? Are you okay?"

"Just a minute."

Was he wrong, or did her voice warble?

He stepped away from the door, then returned to the table and plugged in the flash drive with the security tape. A couple of minutes later, footsteps broke the silence, and Peyton appeared. She looked freshly showered with her wavy hair flowing around her shoulders and accentuating her heart-shaped face. The blue sweater she wore highlighted the sky blue of her eyes and made his pulse clamor with awareness.

Don't go there, man. She's in trouble and needs your help. Not your lustful thoughts.

"How do you feel?" he asked.

"Better. The shower did me a world of good."

She did look calmer, fresh and void of the remnants of the blood on her forehead and her tattered clothing from the night before.

"I was about to review the footage." He pointed out the date.

"This is the night Mama said that strange man came to see her. The one who left me the copy of the drug log." She shivered, and Liam barely resisted pulling her into his arms to console her.

The best way he could help her was to play the footage and see what was on it.

He hit the play button and a grainy tape filled his computer screen. Dammit, the quality was so poor he didn't know if they'd find anything. But he and Peyton watched through the hours of the evening. She identified several cars that came and went as belonging to staff members.

The camera captured Peyton leaving her mother's to go to her place. Liam tensed at the image of a shadowy figure hovering at the side of the building.

He zoomed in on the figure and enlarged it, but the footage was so blurred all he could discern was a pair of work boots and a dark coat with a hood that obliterated the body of the person inside. The figure darted through the bushes along the side of Mrs. Weiss's cottage, veered along the gardens and up the hill toward Peyton's.

Seconds later, a second figure in the gardens caught his eye. A smaller-framed person, hunched in a thin jacket, stooped down by the bench in the garden, head bowed.

His pulse jumped. That figure had stopped at the same spot where Leon's body had been found.

And it was not a man's frame. It was a woman's.

Chapter Seventeen

The fact that the video revealed a woman near Mrs. Weiss's place made Liam wonder if he had it wrong. Could a woman be responsible for attacking Peyton and for the attempt on her mother's life?

"Do you recognize this person?" Liam asked.

Peyton's face paled, and she hesitated a fraction of a second too long. Then she shook her head. "It could be one of the patients or a staff member. Or perhaps a visitor."

Liam narrowed his eyes. She was holding back again. Why?

"If you know who it is, then you need to tell me," he said, hardening his tone. "The only way I can learn the truth is if you're honest with me, Peyton."

She released a wary sigh. "I am being honest. I can't tell who it is from that footage."

A tense heartbeat stretched between them. "Let's look at footage around the time your mother had to be rushed to the ER." He scrolled forward through the night, then to the hours just before dawn and slowed to scrutinize the early morning hours.

No movement on the front, so he shifted and studied the tapes of the back of the property. Nothing there either.

"If someone intentionally caused the gas leak at Mama's, they had to get into the cottage to do it," Peyton said.

Liam snapped his fingers. "True. It could be an inside job—someone who wouldn't look suspicious. I need a list of everyone who works at the Gardens, and anyone involved in your mother's care."

"We can ask the director for a list."

"First, let's look at footage of the rose garden last night." He scrolled through the day before, then to the night and zeroed in on the rose garden. Residents gathered by the pond and gazebo and wandered along the paths weaving through the rows of flower beds. One section held herbs the cook used to add depth to the meals. A few units had full kitchens for the most mobile and mentally cognizant residents who also were welcome to the herbs. But for safety reasons, many only had a microwave and refrigerator.

Peyton went still, and Liam leaned forward to see what she was looking at. Then he spotted a small figure in dark clothing slipping through the garden. Again, a female. But who was she?

She paused by the rose garden near where Leon had been found, then looked back and startled as if she'd heard a noise. Suddenly she bolted and darted into the woods.

Liam wished to hell the film was better quality, but he would send it to the lab and see if they could enhance it and identify the woman.

He scrolled through more footage, searching for Leon Brittles, but the night passed, and the man didn't appear. Dawn came, and the sun rose to streak the sky and mountainside, and the tape suddenly went choppy. Several minutes disappeared before the garden came back into view.

When it did, they watched as a tiny woman in a wheelchair pushed herself onto the path. She bypassed the fountain at the entrance, then seconds later a scream sounded.

Two staff members raced to her from the patio. When they reached the woman, a clear image of Leon lying facedown in the rosebushes appeared.

"What happened?" Peyton asked. "I didn't see anyone after that woman disappeared into the woods. Could someone have been in the rose garden when the film went foggy?"

He gritted his teeth. "Someone tampered with the footage."

He angled himself to study Peyton's face. "Which means it had to be someone who knew about the tapes and had access to them. Someone who works for Golden Gardens."

A SICK FEELING stole through Peyton. She couldn't believe someone at the Gardens was involved in the threats against her and her mother.

Even if that was so, why hurt Leon?

It didn't make sense.

The fact that Val had been in the rose garden the night before he died looked suspicious. But her sister had no motive to hurt him.

She attacked you the other night. Meaning her sister might be desperate and out of control, maybe under the influence of a mood-altering substance. Addiction had changed her personality, and if she'd graduated to more serious narcotics or hallucinogens, she could be psychotic.

"I want to talk to the lady who found Leon," Liam said. "How's her health?"

"She's wheelchair bound due to back issues, but mentally she's pretty sharp."

"Good. I also think we need to canvass the residents to see if anyone has seen anything suspicious."

Peyton gave a nod. "That will be best done on an individual basis in the residents' homes," she said. "Patients who become confused function better in their own surroundings."

"Understood. You should take the lead with them." His keys jangled in his hands.

"First, let's stop by the director's office and ask him to start compiling that list."

She shoved her arms into her jacket, then locked up as they left. Her sister's message about the rose garden taunted her. She had to see what Val had left for her. But she wasn't ready to share her sordid family history with Liam.

He drove them to the main building, and she led him to the director's office. His receptionist announced them, and Director Jameson met them at the door.

"Peyton, I'm so sorry to hear about your mother. How is she doing?"

"Thanks," Peyton said. "She's stable now but unfortunately hasn't regained consciousness."

"I'm keeping her in my prayers." He glanced over her shoulder at Liam. "You must be the federal agent I spoke with a couple of days ago."

Liam offered his hand. "Yes, sir. Special Agent Liam Maverick."

The men exchanged a handshake, then Richard Jameson gestured for them to sit. The director was a tall, dark-haired man, late forties, astute looking with a narrow face and eyes that pinned Liam with a stare.

"Mr. Jameson," Liam began, "there have been several suspicious activities at your facility this past week. First, an attack on Nurse Weiss."

"It is upsetting. I assure you I've done everything possible to beef up security. The safety of our residents and staff is of utmost importance."

"I'm glad to hear you say that," Liam said. "I reviewed security footage for the last few days and found something odd."

The director steepled his hands together. "What's that?"

"The footage during last night is intact, but there are a few minutes where it gets shaky, where I think some time is missing."

A frown furrowed his brows. "I admit our security equipment is outdated. Some of the tapes have been taped over so many times the footage is not as clear as it should be."

Liam murmured a low sound in his throat. "That's an understatement. It also appears that specific tapes have been tampered with, and that makes me suspect someone at Golden Gardens is responsible. I need a list of your current employees as well as ones who've worked here in the past five years."

The man's brows shot up. "Five years?"

"Yes." Liam lifted his chin. "You had one death this morning, another woman almost died yesterday, and

Nurse Weiss has been threatened and attacked on your property. Her mother is also in the hospital fighting for her life because of a suspicious gas leak. If safety is as important as you claim, you'll have no qualms about handing over a list. If for no other reason than for me to clear your people of suspicion."

The director stood and buttoned his jacket. "You have my full cooperation. I'll have my assistant start compiling that list and get it to you ASAP."

Liam stood and gave a clipped nod. "Thank you."

Peyton's head swam as they left the office. She knew every person who worked at the Gardens. Was friendly with most of them. They'd done team-building exercises together, shared funny and sad stories about their patients and supported each other during personal crises. Devoted to making Golden Gardens a happy, homelike atmosphere, not a grim place where people went to die, the staff planned special activities for the residents, including holiday parties, craft fairs, a gardening club for those interested in maintaining the gardens, and they'd formed a cooking club. On special occasions they even brought in entertainment.

She couldn't imagine any one of them trying to hurt her or her mother.

ALTHOUGH PEYTON INSISTED she trusted each and every staff member employed at Golden Gardens, Liam had to keep an open mind.

Something wasn't right in this place. He could feel it. And Peyton was at the center.

How it all tied back to Gloria Inman's death and the hospital fire, he didn't know yet. But he wouldn't give up until he did.

She directed him to Ms. Marley's cottage and led him up the sidewalk. "Ms. Marley lives in the midcare section where assistance with daily living is needed, but not necessarily memory care. Some residents respond better to a more social environment and having a roommate. Ms. Marley is one of them. Her unit has two bedrooms with a common living area and a partial kitchen."

Peyton knocked, and a twentyish young woman in scrubs answered the door.

"Hi, Lorrie," Peyton said. "How's Ms. Marley doing?"

"Better now she had some rest. She was pretty shaken up this morning."

"Understandably so." Peyton introduced Liam, then explained to Liam that Lorrie was a nurse's assistant who often sat with patients in need.

"We need to talk to her about what happened," Peyton said softly.

Lorrie gave a little nod, her blond ponytail swinging as she waved them into the small foyer. "I just fixed her some hot tea," Lorrie said. "And I encouraged her to eat some toast. She wasn't hungry this morning."

Finding a dead body could kill one's appetite.

Knowing the woman would be more comfortable with Peyton than him, Liam gestured for her to take the lead. Watching her give the elderly woman a hug and gently rub her back stirred Liam's admiration.

"Ms. Marley, a friend of mine wants to ask you some questions about when you found Leon."

Ms. Marley's hands shook as she set down her china teacup. "Did I do something wrong?"

"No, of course not," Peyton assured her. "It's just routine. He's going talk to the other residents, as well.

We just want to find out exactly what happened to Leon."

"He's dead, that's what happened to him," Ms. Marley said.

Liam bit back a smile at the woman's snappy tone. He bet this lady had been a handful in her younger years. Hell, she probably still was.

Liam seated himself across from her and offered her a smile. "Did you see Leon this morning at any time before you found him in the garden?"

"No," Ms. Marley said, then tore her toast into small bites.

"What about last night?" Liam asked.

A thoughtful expression colored her face. "We played cards in the evening after dinner. But the old geezer cheated, and I told him so, then left."

"Was anyone else playing cards with you?" Liam asked.

She bit her lip, and Liam knew she was hiding something. "Who else was there?"

"No one." She leaned forward and spoke in a whisper. "It was a date, just me and Leon, but Gertie Sommers likes Leon and gets jealous, so we were sneaking around." She rolled her eyes. "This place is a pure gossip mill."

Liam coughed to keep from laughing at her comment. "Do you think Gertie knew about you two anyway?"

"Oh, my word, you don't think Gertie would kill Leon because he was seeing me, do you?"

That hadn't occurred to him. Maybe he should ask if Gertie had an alibi.

"Do *you* think that?" Liam asked.

Ms. Marley pursed her lips. "Heavens no. She's a mousy busybody, but she plays around, too. Leon isn't the only man she wants here."

He glanced at Peyton and saw amusement in her eyes.

"I see." Liam hesitated. "So, tell me what happened this morning."

"I got up to go for my morning walk," Ms. Marley said, then shrugged at the wheelchair. "I mean my stroll. I'm part of the gardening club and wanted to make sure we didn't need to prune the roses today. Sometimes Leon and I meet our friends for coffee, but he wasn't on the patio, so I decided to wait for him to have breakfast, so I headed out to the garden. I'd just checked the herbs when I spotted his legs sticking out of the rosebushes." Her face paled again, and she dabbed at a tear. "I knew it was him the minute I saw his mismatched socks. He was color blind you know."

Liam coughed into his hand. "Then what happened?"

"I started shouting and everyone came running. Well, that is, the staff did. Not many of us here can run anymore." She chuckled at her own comment. "I so hate that he's gone. It's hard to find a good man at my age. Especially one who's good at cards."

Liam smiled again. "Did you see anyone else in the garden this morning? Maybe someone out by the woods or the pond?"

She shook her head no, then adjusted her tiny wire-rimmed glasses. "Everyone else was gathering on the patio. But then, I don't see too good these days."

Liam laid a business card on the table. "If you think of anything else, please call me."

"Maybe Mr. Leon simply died of natural causes," Peyton said as they left.

Liam shrugged. "Or maybe he saw something he shouldn't have seen. Like the person who tried to kill your mother."

Peyton's pained look made him feel like hell. But he couldn't sugarcoat the facts and protect her at the same time. She obviously trusted everyone who worked here, but he didn't.

If someone at the Gardens was a killer, she needed to be on guard every minute.

PEYTON HATED TO BE suspicious of the people she worked with. But if Liam was right, a killer could be hiding among them, and no one was safe.

They spent the next two hours visiting and questioning each of the residents. Liam was fishing for information on the staff members and subtly inquired about problems or mistreatment.

The few residents who remembered Miller Conrad gushed that he was a compassionate PA who took extra time to make them comfortable and cared for. Many of the residents had lost loved ones and were alone, leaving them with few to no visitors.

Liam received a text from his brother requesting they meet at the sheriff's office, so they drove there after finishing the interviews. Dread filled Peyton when she saw his brother's face.

"Come on back." Sheriff Maverick led to the same interrogation room where they'd brought her before.

A man sat at the table, wearing a lab coat, square glasses, his sandy-brown hair combed neatly off his forehead. A file sat in front of him, his hand placed on top.

The sheriff gestured for her and Liam to sit, and they did. Judging from the sheriff's body language, he had disturbing news. Liam introduced her to Dr. Hammerhead, the ME.

"Brantley is in the other room," the sheriff told Liam. "I was just about to question him, when he arrived."

Dr. Hammerhead adjusted his glasses, then opened the file. "I have the results of Mrs. Inman's autopsy."

Sheriff Maverick folded his arms. "It doesn't look good, Peyton. This report indicates that you gave the woman a lethal dose of morphine."

Chapter Eighteen

Tension knotted Peyton's stomach. She'd sensed something wasn't right in the ER, and then when Dr. Butler had shown her that drug log.

"I explained that to Liam," Peyton said. "I did not give Mrs. Inman morphine."

Liam's jaw tightened. "What did you find, Dr. Hammerhead?"

Dr. Hammerhead cleared his throat. "Cause of death was heart failure due to cardiac arrest." He gestured to the file. "But the cause of the heart issue is what's interesting."

Liam stiffened. "What caused it?"

"I'm getting to that." Dr. Hammerhead rubbed a hand down his face. "The toxicology report indicates that Mrs. Inman had large amounts of opioids in her system." He glanced at Peyton. "Was the hospital aware of that when she was brought in?"

Peyton shook her head. "No. The only medications Mr. Inman listed were blood pressure medicine and a statin for high cholesterol."

The lines on the ME's forehead crinkled. "The autopsy indicates she was a long-term user—abuser."

Peyton's mind raced. "But Mr. Inman never mentioned a history of drug use."

"Maybe he didn't know," Liam suggested.

Some people hid their addiction from friends and family. Val had at first, until the situation had gotten out of control and had taken over her life.

"An overdose of opioids could have affected her heart and triggered her to go into arrest," Peyton said.

"Exactly." The ME held up a finger. "But there's more. According to the tox report, she was given morphine within a half hour before her death. Which would mean she received it in the hospital."

Peyton shook her head. "We did not administer morphine or any pain meds when she came in. We were assessing her condition and I gave her a shot of epinephrine."

"One shot?" Dr. Hammerhead asked.

Peyton tensed. "Yes, why do you ask?"

Dr. Hammerhead removed his glasses. "Because there were two injection sites and double the amount of epinephrine in her system."

"That makes no sense," Peyton muttered. "Unless someone else gave her a shot before I did. But we record every aspect of the treatment so mistakes like that don't happen in the ER."

"Except, according to the log report," Sheriff Maverick said, "your code was used to check out both morphine and the epinephrine."

Peyton went cold inside as she glanced at Liam. She knew exactly how it looked. Just like Dr. Butler had said it would.

It either appeared she'd made a mistake in the ER, or she had killed Gloria Inman.

She gripped the chair with clammy hands. "Is this the point where I ask for an attorney?"

Liam and Jacob exchanged furtive looks. "Do you need one?" Jacob asked.

Peyton's lungs strained for air. "I don't know. I haven't done anything wrong, but I'm not naive enough to believe that my word is enough when evidence points to the contrary."

It was one reason she hadn't come forward sooner.

LIAM DIDN'T BELIEVE that Peyton was responsible for any of this. But he also couldn't discount facts.

Those facts needed to be backed by motive which Peyton lacked. She certainly seemed competent enough not to inject a patient with the wrong meds or too much medication. And paperwork could be doctored.

He wished to hell he had autopsies on the three other patients who died where Miller Conrad had worked.

"Let's get the autopsy for Leon Brittles," Liam said. "The tox report should tell us if he had opioids or epinephrine in his system."

"You need a list of his regular medications for comparison," Peyton said.

"The ME will handle that," Liam said.

Although if someone had gone to the trouble to frame Peyton and the same person had killed Leon, and they worked at the Gardens, they could have tampered with his medical records.

Jacob gestured toward the door. "Let's go talk to Brantley."

"Wait here," Liam told Peyton. "I'll drive you to the hospital when I'm finished."

Peyton pulled her phone from her purse. "I'll call and check on Mama."

Liam gave a little nod, then followed Jacob from the room, into the hall. They crossed to Interrogation Room 2 and entered.

Herbert Brantley sat scowling, his hands knotted on top of the table, his shoulders rigid.

"Why the hell am I here?"

Jacob dropped a folder on the desk, then sank into the chair across from the man. Liam remained standing, arms crossed as he leaned against the wall.

"You worked at Whistler Hospital five years ago," Jacob began. "You were on duty the night Gloria Inman died."

Brantley shifted. "So were a lot of other hospital staff members."

"True." Jacob tapped the file. "But not all of them have a record for selling drugs."

The man's breath wheezed out. "That was a long time ago. I was practically a kid."

"Yet now you work in a field where you have access to opioids and narcotics on a daily basis."

"I work in a field to *help* people," Brantley said. "And for the record, I don't know what happened to Mrs. Inman. Why don't you ask that nurse who was in the ER with her? Maybe she screwed up."

Liam didn't like the fact that he was so quick to point suspicion toward Peyton. "You were also on duty the night of the hospital fire."

Brantley's eyes flared with anger. "If you're suggesting I had something to do with that fire, you're wrong."

Jacob let the silence stand for a minute, and Brantley shifted again, then flexed his fingers.

"Where were you last night and early this morning?"

"Home. In bed asleep," Brantley said flatly.

"Can anyone verify that?" Jacob asked.

A seed of panic flared in the man's eyes. "No, I was alone. Why? Do I need an alibi?"

"A patient at Golden Gardens died in the night," Jacob said. "Leon Brittles."

"I have no idea who he is, so why would I hurt him?"

"Money," Liam suggested. "You never did explain how you bought all those things we asked you about."

"And I don't have to," Brantley said.

Liam didn't like this bastard. He had to keep pushing him.

"Where were you night before last?"

Brantley jiggled his leg. "Had the night off so I went to a bar."

"I'll need to know the name of that bar."

Brantley worked his mouth from side to side.

"Let's talk about the night Gloria Inman died again." He tapped the tabletop. "Did you know Mrs. Inman had a large number of opioids in her system when she was admitted to the hospital?"

Brantley folded his arms. "How would I know? I wasn't in the ER with her."

"I have a search warrant for your house and belongings," Liam interjected. "Am I going to find opioids there?"

Brantley went stone still. "I'm done talking. I want a lawyer."

"All right." Liam glared down at him. "But if you started that hospital fire and had anything to do with these other people's deaths, no lawyer will be able to save you. You're going to rot in prison for the rest of your life."

PEYTON ASKED TO speak to the head nurse in charge of her mother's room, who turned out to be a kind older woman named Letty Hutchins. "Your mother's condition is the same. Her vitals are good, but she still hasn't regained consciousness."

That worried Peyton the most.

"Did the doctor run a full blood panel?"

"Yes, when she first arrived. He's ordered a CAT scan and an MRI for this afternoon."

"Good." She worried her bottom lip with her teeth as she thought about the oddity with Mrs. Inman's toxicology report.

"I'll be there in a few minutes," Peyton told the nurse. "Please call me if there's a change."

"I will."

Just as Peyton ended the call, her phone dinged. Joanna. She pressed Connect. "Hey, Jo."

"I just talked to the director." Worry laced Joanna's tone. "What's going on, Peyton? He said that federal agent wants a list of all the employees at the Gardens. He can't possibly think someone here hurt Leon or your mother."

He thought exactly that. "He's covering all the bases. Something's going on at the Gardens, Jo. First my mother, then Leon."

A heartbeat of silence passed. "Your mama is going to make it," Jo assured her.

Tears clogged Peyton's throat. "I hope so." She mentally debated how much to share. Jo had been her best friend, ever since she'd moved to Golden Gardens. "Jo, I called Agent Maverick because someone threatened me."

"What?"

She quickly explained about the threat after Mrs. Inman's death. "That's the reason I moved Mama to Golden Gardens. I was afraid for her."

"Oh my God, Peyton. I had no idea," Joanna said softly. "You should have told me."

"There's more. Agent Maverick exhumed Gloria Inman's body, and the ME performed another autopsy. According to him, Gloria had opioids in her system and received two shots of epinephrine."

"That doesn't sound right."

"It's not. Mr. Inman claims his wife didn't take opioids and I didn't give her a double dose of the epinephrine or any morphine. But someone is trying to make it look like I did."

Joanna gasped. "Who would do such a thing?"

"I don't know for sure. But Agent Maverick is questioning two men who are persons of interest. A med tech and a PA."

"I don't understand," Joanna said.

"Neither do I," Peyton said. "But Dr. Butler could be involved. Whatever is going on, there definitely was some kind of cover-up with Mrs. Inman's death, and the agent believes that case is related to the hospital fire, that it was set to destroy evidence of wrongdoing."

"This is hard to believe," Joanna said. "Dr. Butler seems so conscientious. And I know you are."

"I'm scared, Jo." Peyton gulped back a sob.

"It's going to be okay, Pey. But I'm so sorry you got caught up in this. No wonder you didn't want your mother left alone for a minute."

Emotions churned inside Peyton, and she willed her mother to pull through.

Every minute she remained unconscious intensified her worry that she might not wake up at all.

JACOB ESCORTED AN irate Brantley to a holding cell. They could hold him for twenty-four hours without charging him, and they intended to do so. A night in jail might persuade him to open up. If the man was addicted to opioids himself, he would be getting antsy for a fix. It also would give them time to search his house and car.

In light of the autopsy results on Gloria Inman, Jacob escorted Barry Inman back into the interrogation room. Inman looked more rested than he had when they'd first brought him in. Living off the grid had its drawbacks. Here he'd been given three hot meals and a bed to sleep in.

It probably felt like a hotel compared to how he'd lived the last five years.

"Well, Mr. Inman," Liam said as Jacob closed the door. "We need to have another chat."

Inman rocked back in the chair. "I hope you're going to tell me I'm being released. That you know what happened to my wife, and that you arrested the real person who set that fire."

"Actually, we know a little more about what happened to your wife, but no, we're not ready to release you just yet," Liam said.

Inman's eyes turned feral. "Cut to the chase then."

Jacob dropped a folder with a copy of the ME's findings on the table. "We have the results of your wife's autopsy."

Inman went still, the legs of the chair hitting the floor with a thud. "Then you know I was telling the truth. That the hospital made a mistake."

Liam chewed the inside of his cheek as he scrutinized Inman's reaction. "There was a mistake, yes. But we're not sure of the source."

Inman exhaled noisily. "Stop beating around the bush. What caused my wife's death?"

"Cause of death was cardiac arrest," Liam said. "But there were oddities in the tox report. According to the hospital staff, you did not disclose the fact that your wife was addicted to opioids when you brought her to the ER."

The color drained from Inman's face. "What are you talking about? My wife didn't do drugs. And she certainly wasn't an addict."

The ME checked her medical history for injuries or chronic pain. But he wanted to hear Inman's response. "Did your wife suffer any injuries lately or in the past few years?"

"No, nothing like that."

"How about chronic back pain?" Liam asked.

"No." Inman lurched up and slapped his hands on the table. "This is crazy. My wife was not an addict."

Liam glanced at Jacob, and he shrugged. "I hate to tell you this, but the autopsy proves long-term abuse. Perhaps she hid it from you."

Inman shook his head in denial. "I can't believe this. Gloria was doing drugs…"

"She either took or was given morphine shortly before her death. The ME also found two injection sites where she received epinephrine. The nurse who treated her denies giving her morphine or more than one injection of epi."

Inman scowled. "Then she's lying."

"I don't think so," Liam answered. "Do you know what epinephrine does to the body, Mr. Inman?"

He shrugged. "I know it's used for people with allergies."

"Right. It's also given when a person's heart stops. It's a stimulant which jump-starts the heart. But given to a patient who doesn't need it, it can trigger a heart attack."

Inman ran a hand over his eyes. "You're saying the nurse killed her with epinephrine?"

Liam shook his head. "No, I think someone else injected her, maybe before she went to the hospital. That shot triggered her to go into cardiac arrest."

Inman shook his head again, then cursed. "No... I did not kill Gloria." He balled his hands into fists. "I didn't. You have to believe me."

The trouble was, Liam was starting to.

But if Inman hadn't injected his wife with drugs, who had?

Chapter Nineteen

"Mr. Inman," Jacob cut in. "We're aware that you and the woman you had an affair with work for a pharmaceutical company where you have access to a variety of drugs. Are you sure you didn't supply your wife with opioids?"

Inman's eyes flared with bitterness. "I'm sure. Besides, our samples are carefully monitored to prevent anyone from skimming them from the company. There's no way I could have done that without getting caught and losing my job." His breath hitched. "And if I'd thought my wife had a problem, I would have insisted she get help, not feed her habit."

"Then we won't find any opioids at your house?" Jacob asked.

Confusion marred Inman's expression. "I don't think so. But if you're saying Gloria abused drugs, and I didn't have a clue, it's possible she had a hidden stash." He scrubbed a hand down his face. "I can't believe this is happening."

"What about epinephrine? Do you have access to it through your company?"

Inman shook his head. "Everything the company is

doing is experimental. Drugs to treat cancer patients and…" His voice faded.

"And what else?" Liam asked.

Inman's face paled. "And Alzheimer's."

"Which would be used in an assisted-living and nursing facility," Liam pointed out.

Inman dropped his head forward. "I didn't drug Gloria or anyone else. I swear to God I didn't."

If he was innocent, Liam might feel sorry for the guy. But he couldn't discount him as a suspect yet.

"If you think of anything else that might be helpful, let me know." Jacob gestured for him to stand. "Meanwhile, you're gonna be with us a little while longer."

Inman looked panicked. "You have to find the truth. Someone may be setting me up."

Liam gave him a blank look. "That's exactly what we think happened with Nurse Weiss."

Inman shuffled beside Jacob, protesting his innocence as Jacob led him back to his cell.

"What next?" Jacob asked.

"Search his house. I'm going to drive Peyton to the hospital to see her mother. And I intend to have a chat with Dr. Butler."

The man had either protected Peyton regarding Mrs. Inman's death, or he was the one who'd framed her to take the fall if police investigated.

He texted Bennett and asked him to find everything he could on the doctor.

While you're at it, research the director of Golden Gardens.

If something was wrong at the facility, Director Jameson might know more than he was saying.

PEYTON CHEWED HER FINGERNAIL as Liam drove to the hospital. As a little girl, she'd been a nail biter. Her mother had tried everything to break the habit, but it hadn't worked. After college, she'd begun painting her nails because she found if they were polished, she tended not to chew on them.

She looked down and noted the polish was in shambles now, and she'd nearly chewed her thumbnail to the quick.

"Inman denies everything, even knowing that his wife took opioids," Liam said as he rounded a curve. "In light of this new information, I want to question Dr. Butler again and find out if he's really your friend or the enemy."

Peyton's mind raced to assimilate everything they'd learned. She felt as if they were on a Tilt-A-Whirl where everything kept shifting and they were spinning in circles. She wanted to get off and have her feet on solid ground, but the Tilt-A-Whirl was gaining momentum instead of slowing.

"I'm going to review my mother's medical chart," she told Liam. "The fact that she hadn't regained consciousness worries me." She picked at a cuticle. "Typically, I trust hospital staff, but now I don't know what to think."

Liam covered her hand with his. "I don't blame you. It's best to keep your eyes wide open right now until we know who's behind this."

He pulled into the hospital visitors' lot and parked, then gave her hand another squeeze. "Hang in there, Peyton. I think we're getting closer."

Her heart stuttered at the tenderness in his eyes and voice. She latched on to his words and their gazes locked. Liam Maverick was not just an agent, but a virile and understanding man. She wondered why he wasn't married with a family of his own.

Although perhaps he had a girlfriend or lover.

It doesn't matter. He's with you to solve a case, not get romantic.

The thought sobered her, and she dragged her gaze away and climbed from the car. They walked in silence up to the hospital entrance. Like a gentleman, he opened the door for her. She hurried to the elevator, her pulse pounding. Maybe hearing her voice would bring her mother back to life.

While Liam spoke to the deputy stationed outside her mother's room, a heavy fear fell over Peyton. Eyes closed, unmoving, her mother looked so pale and fragile that Peyton rushed to her to make sure she was still breathing.

Her hand felt cold and clammy, and her chest rose and fell slowly. Thank God she was alive. But she was struggling.

She leaned over and kissed her mother's cheek. "I'm here, Mama. Please wake up. I need to see your bright, shining eyes." And know that I'm not alone.

She stared at her mother's face, willing her to make some movement, to open her eyes and look at her. To say something.

She squeezed her pale, limp hand. But nothing happened.

Tears threatened to choke her. "Come on. You have to fight. It's not your time yet."

Although fear that she was wrong needled at Peyton. What if it was her mother's time? What if she lost her? How would she go on?

LIAM HAD TO WAIT on Dr. Butler to finish a consult before he could question him. The man looked annoyed as Liam studied the diplomas, awards and certificates on his wall. Dr. Butler had graduated from Brody School of Medicine at East Carolina University, then did his residency at UNC in Chapel Hill.

"My time is limited, Agent Maverick," Dr. Butler said curtly. "Get on with it."

Liam seated himself across from the physician. "I had an interesting conversation with Peyton Weiss. She explained that she'd withheld the truth about the night Gloria Inman died."

Dr. Butler rolled a pen between his fingers.

"She admitted that she voiced concerns to you, but you produced paperwork indicating she was at fault. She denies giving Mrs. Inman opioids, and states that she gave her one shot of epinephrine."

"All I can tell you is what that log report showed."

Liam narrowed his eyes. "You were in that ER with her," he said. "Didn't you know what meds were dispensed?"

"I gave the order for the epi," Dr. Butler said. "If Nurse Weiss gave Mrs. Inman an opioid or a second epi shot, I didn't see her do it."

"Then how do you explain that log?"

His eyes widened. "I can't. All I know is that her code was used to open the medicine cart."

Liam hesitated. The doctor sounded convincing. But some people were adept at lying. And he could have told himself this story so many times that he'd actually started believing it himself.

"Dr. Butler, is it possible that someone else could have gotten hold of Peyton's code?"

He tapped his pen on the desk. "The staff are instructed not to share codes. If Peyton shared hers, then she's responsible for whatever drugs were removed."

"What if she didn't share it? What if someone stole it or found out on their own?"

"You'll have to ask Peyton if she left it somewhere that someone could have gotten hold of it."

"You encouraged her not to talk to the police," Liam said.

"Listen, Agent Maverick, I think highly of Nurse Weiss. She's dedicated, hardworking, compassionate and giving. I wish we had a thousand more just like her. That's the reason I told her to keep quiet. I didn't want her reputation ruined over a mistake."

Liam leaned forward. "But didn't you want to know what happened?"

The man's expression went flat. "Yes, of course I did. But we did everything possible to save the woman, and sometimes we fail."

Liam swallowed. "Maybe you weren't concerned about Peyton's reputation. Maybe it was your own you wanted to save."

Dr. Butler's expression turned steely.

"Then you were worried she would talk to the police, so that night you called and threatened her."

"What?" Outrage sharpened his features. "What are you talking about?"

"Peyton says a man phoned her and threatened her.

He told her that if she didn't keep quiet, her mother would end up like Gloria Inman."

The doctor rolled his hands into fists, then unfolded one and reached for the phone. "We're finished, Agent Maverick. If you want to speak to me again, you'll have to go through my attorney."

Liam had expected him to lawyer up. But he didn't like it.

"You can hide behind a lawyer if you want, Doc. But we also believe that whoever threatened Peyton attacked her. And we think that same person caused the gas leak that sent her mother to the ER. If she dies, that's going to constitute a homicide."

He stood, gave the man a lethal stare, then left him sweating as he punched his lawyer's number.

PEYTON CHECKED HER MOTHER'S medical record, but nothing seemed amiss. Was she paranoid?

No, something nefarious was going on.

She pressed a cool washcloth to her mother's face, gently wiping her eyes. *Please wake up, Mama.*

But she showed no reaction.

Despair threatened, but she reminded herself she'd seen patients who were unresponsive for days, even weeks, suddenly regain consciousness and recover. She had to think positive.

"Remember when you used to sing to me and Val," she whispered. "And dance. I always liked it when you cranked up the music and sang and danced around the kitchen." A smile tugged at her lips. "Val and I used to hide out in the hall and watch you." She stroked her mother's soft gray curls away from her forehead. "We used to giggle and laugh. Sometimes we made fun of your moves, but we didn't mean any harm, Mama." Tears filled her eyes. "We loved it." She swiped at a tear that found its way down her cheek. "I remember one time you caught us, and you dragged us all in the kitchen and we held hands and danced together. I think I was ten and Val was eight." Her voice choked. "I'll never forget that night. Never." It was a time when they were innocent and she and her sister were close, and life seemed full of fun and promises.

Her mother had been strong and had taught her and Val to be. Until Val hit fourteen and everything went south.

Peyton silently chastised herself for the millionth time. At sixteen, she'd just discovered boys and a seventeen-year-old soccer player had actually shown interest in her. She'd been so caught up in young love that she'd been oblivious to the fact that her sister had started slipping away into depression. Val had been the beautiful one, the outgoing girl, the athletic one with the long, lithe body. Even at fourteen, Val had drawn the eyes of the older boys. Peyton had been envious of her confidence and grace.

She was the shyer one. The bookworm. The one who didn't quite know how to dress.

Then Seth Simmons had asked her to homecoming.

That night while she'd received her first kiss, Val had almost OD'd.

Pain wrenched her at the memory. She'd felt guilty for not knowing her sister was in pain and had devoted the next few months to making sure Val felt loved and cared for.

But Val had never been the same. And neither had their relationship.

Guilt had sent her to a therapist who helped her deal with her emotions. Eventually she'd chosen nursing as a career—maybe to make up for the one person she couldn't save.

Her mother's body suddenly jerked and spasmed, and Peyton jumped up and checked the monitors. Oxygen saturation level low. Blood pressure dropping. Heart monitor beeping wildly.

Machines beeped and sounded, and a flood of nurses and doctors rushed inside. She backed away, praying as they began CPR again.

Her own heart thundered, her lungs straining for air. One of the nurses coaxed her into the hallway. The deputy outside the door clutched her arm to steady her.

Liam appeared, his brows knitted. "Peyton?"

"She's coding," Peyton whispered.

A sob wrenched from her gut, and her legs buckled. Liam wrapped his arms around her and caught her, then held her to him as she watched the staff work to save her mother.

The next half hour passed in a blur. Fear, panic and a surreal feeling overcame her, but Liam continued to hold her and soothe her with soft words. Finally, the doctor emerged from the room, his expression grim.

"She's alive, but she lapsed into a coma," he said, his voice filled with compassion.

"Will she recover?" Peyton asked, although she knew the answer. He didn't know. Only time would tell. It could be hours, days, weeks, months…

He cleared his throat. "We'll run a test to check her brain activity if you want."

"Let's give her tonight," she murmured. "If she hasn't responded by morning, you can run the tests."

"Understood."

One of the nurses remained, and Peyton stepped inside and rushed to her mother. Liam gave the deputy a break while Peyton held her mother's hand.

Hours later when she could hardly keep her eyes open, he rubbed her back.

"This may go on for days, Peyton. You have to rest sometime," he said softly. "Let me drive you home."

She nodded, although rest was the last thing on her mind. If the person who'd threatened her had hurt her mother, she had to find the bastard.

Val had left something important for her in that rose garden. She needed to find out what it was.

Chapter Twenty

Worry for Peyton nagged at Liam. She lapsed into silence as he drove her back to Golden Gardens.

Although she stared out the window, he sensed she wasn't really looking at anything. That her mind was filled with fear.

The quarter moon fought through the storm clouds above, barely managing to break through. He searched for stars, but they were shrouded by the clouds and darkness. A car raced up on his tail, and he checked the rearview mirror, his instincts on alert.

He rounded a curve and veered onto a side road. The car followed. Dammit. "Hang on."

She sat up straighter and glanced over her shoulder. "We're being followed."

"I don't know. Maybe." He pressed the accelerator and sped down the curvy road, then made another turn. The car turned right behind him, then suddenly raced around him. He braced himself for impact if the car tried to run him off the road, but tires squealed, and the car sped on. Liam tried to read the license plate, but there wasn't one. The car was black, a sedan, nondescript. A hundred just like them everywhere you looked.

Peyton released a shaky breath. "He went on."

"Because he realized I made him," Liam said.

Fear shadowed her face. "I don't understand why this is all happening."

Liam reached across the console and rubbed her shoulder. "I know. But we're going to get to the truth. I promise."

She gave a small nod, although she didn't look convinced. She looked exhausted and weary and so damn vulnerable that his heart gave a pang.

He maneuvered the next turn, wound down the long drive to the security gate for Golden Gardens, then drove to Peyton's apartment. Her breathing sounded choppy as she climbed from the vehicle and walked to her door. Liam followed close behind, scanning the property.

He urged Peyton to wait in the foyer while he searched her apartment. It didn't take him long to do a walk-through. "Everything looks fine," he said as he returned to the living room. She stood looking at a photograph of her and her mother taken among the spring tulips in the garden. Peyton looked at peace there, and beautiful with the sunshine slanting across her heart-shaped face.

Unlike now. A tear trickled down the side of her cheek, and her body shook with emotions. Liam couldn't resist. He crossed the room to her and drew her into his arms. She leaned into him and buried her head against his chest. Her pain bled through to him, and he stroked her back and murmured soft, soothing words as she purged her emotions.

Finally, her breathing steadied, and she looked up at him. "I'm sorry."

He gently feathered a strand of her hair from her cheek. "It's okay. You're going through a rough time."

"I don't usually fall apart," she said quietly.

He tilted her chin up with his thumb and gave her a small smile. "It's understandable. I know you're worried sick about your mother."

"I am." She swallowed hard. "She has to be all right."

He wished he could promise her that she would survive. But he wasn't a doctor, and her health had apparently been fragile before the gas leak sent her to the ER.

She blinked away more tears. "You're pretty understanding for an FBI agent."

He chuckled. "Thanks. I think."

Her gaze met his, and heat flared between them. She laid her hand against his cheek. "I meant it. You're strong and tough, but you've been amazingly understanding to me, Liam."

"You're a compassionate woman, Peyton. One who helps other people. It's time someone took care of you for a change."

"I can't imagine what that would be like," she said softly.

Liam lowered his head and kissed her hair, then pulled her into his arms and held her. He couldn't make false promises, but he would show her what it was like to be taken care of, at least for a little while.

PEYTON CLOSED HER EYES, savoring the comfort of Liam's strong, protective arms. His tender kiss in her hair stirred a deep longing to be touched and loved in a way she hadn't in a long time. Maybe forever.

When was the last time she'd been with a man? Allowed one into her heart? Her bed?

Maybe college. But Val's addiction had gotten in the

way then. The guy she'd been dating hadn't wanted to be linked to a girl with family problems.

So, she'd shut herself off from men. Figured they'd all feel the same way.

Then the incident at the hospital with Gloria Inman happened. She'd tried to be strong afterward. Had suppressed the pain from her sister's addiction, and from watching her mother deteriorate.

She looked into Liam's eyes, expecting censure. Instead understanding and concern darkened his eyes. Other emotions glittered there, as well. Ones she didn't know how to put a name on. Tomorrow they'd continue the case, hopefully find the truth.

Tonight, she wanted him to hold her and to pretend that everything was all right.

She traced her finger along his square jaw, and he clenched it, heat flaring across his face.

"Peyton?"

In the morning, she might regret what she was about to do, but need and desire emboldened her, and she stood on tiptoe and pressed her lips to his. For the briefest of seconds, he hesitated, and she thought he wasn't going to kiss her.

She moved her lips gently against his, and he sighed and cupped her face between his hands. His lips bonded with hers, gliding across her mouth in a sensual foray, making her breath quicken. Need thundered through her, and she traced her tongue along his lips, pleading for more.

He slid one hand to her waist and pulled her into the vee of his thighs as he plunged his tongue into her mouth. Her body tingled with desire, and she threaded her fingers into his thick hair. He groaned, and she moved her body against him. Her nipples stiffened to turgid peaks, liquid heat pooling in her belly.

His lips teased hers, his tongue trailed a line down her throat and she threw her head back, feeling wild and needy and ready to abandon caution. Together they kissed and teased each other until the titillating sensations built inside her, and she raked her hands down the corded muscles of his back.

His sex hardened, pressing into her heat, stirring her passion to a frenzy. She hadn't been naked with a man in over five years. Had forgotten what it felt like to be held and kissed and touched so sensually.

She didn't want the feeling to end. She wanted him in her bed loving her all night.

Her hands dropped to his chest and she slowly began unbuttoning his shirt. He groaned her name, then trailed kisses along her neck, dipping lower to tease her breasts through her blouse. She sighed her pleasure, then freed the top half of his shirt and ran her hands inside to feel his bare skin. A soft sprinkling of dark hair covered his broad chest, and his hips shifted, his sex stroking her heat.

She pushed at his shirt, anxious to feel his body against hers and pressed a kiss to his muscled chest. His skin tasted salty and manly, making her crave more of him.

But when she reached for his belt, he placed his hand over hers. "Peyton, stop."

Hurt stole her breath, and she dropped her hands. "I'm sorry. I...shouldn't have been so bold." For heaven's sake, he'd simply been comforting her, and she'd read too much into it because she was lonely and needy.

No, it wasn't just that. She had been attracted to

the sexy man ever since she'd met him. And she admired him.

She might even be falling for him.

But he didn't want her, so she stepped away.

IT TOOK EVERY OUNCE of restraint Liam had not to throw Peyton onto the couch and tear her clothes off. She was a vixen in disguise.

He couldn't remember the last time a woman had him panting and desperate for a hot night between the sheets with her. But Peyton made him want that and more.

The very reason he had to end this madness.

Her cheeks reddened as she started toward the bedroom, but he caught her arm and forced her to look at him. His breathing was erratic, his heart hammering, his body pulsing with desire.

"Peyton, let me set the record straight. I'm the one who should apologize. I'm supposed to protect you, not jump your bones."

A frown crinkled her forehead. "You didn't jump my bones. I started this. But it's obvious you don't want me."

He took her hand and pressed it over his throbbing sex. "Make no mistake. I want you all right. I think you're a brave, smart, amazing woman. But I can't take advantage of you." He caressed her cheek with the back of his hand. "You're beautiful and desirable, but you're hurting and frightened, and I don't want you to hate me in the morning."

Emotions glittered in Peyton's eyes. "I understand."

Then she turned and fled into her room and shut the door. Liam walked to the sliding glass doors and looked out at the inky sky. The wind rustled leaves and trees, the sound oddly calming and eerie at the same time.

The mountains beyond rose with sharp ridges and dangers, the dense woods a perfect place for a predator to hide. Was someone out there watching Peyton? Waiting for her to be alone so he could strike?

In the bedroom, he heard footsteps, then saw a light flicker off and imagined Peyton crawling into bed alone.

His body throbbed with need. His heart ached to put a smile on her face. His arms begged to hold her all night.

But his mind whispered that if he did, he'd be crossing the line. His own rules echoed in his head. Never get involved with a suspect or a witness. Keep your professional and personal life separate.

Guard your heart.

Loving someone and losing them hurt too damn much. And if he allowed his emotions to lead him, he might fail on the job.

Peyton needed him to be on his *A* game until she was safe.

His phone buzzed. Jacob.

Grateful for the intrusion to get his libido under control, he pressed Connect and stepped outside on the patio for fresh air. "Jacob?"

"Yeah. We searched Inman's house and guess what we found."

"Opioids?"

"A stash full. Mostly oxy and hydrocodone."

"The husband said she wasn't taking any."

"Either he's lying, or the poor idiot really was oblivious to the fact that his wife had an addiction."

"Some people hide it well," Liam said.

"They do. I'll show the pills to him in the morning and gauge his reaction."

"Were they black market or prescribed?"

"A little of both. There are three different prescribers listed on the scripts, so I'll look into that angle. If we're dealing with a pill mill, we need to shut it down."

The ever-growing problem of opioid addiction. Shut one pill mill or dealer down and another one cropped up the next day. Could it be linked to Gloria's death? And the threats against Peyton?

The discrepancy between the drug log and Peyton's statement might indicate it was.

Liam relayed his conversation with Dr. Butler and the fact that he'd lawyered up, then filled him in on Mrs. Weiss's condition.

"Sorry to hear she's not doing well," Jacob said. "Oh, gotta go. Cora was having some back pain earlier, so I want to be close in case she goes into labor."

"Text us if she does, man. You know we all want to be there."

Jacob muttered he would, then hung up. Liam's heart clenched. He was happy for his brothers. But dammit, now he was starting to want a family of his own. Peyton's face taunted him.

Don't go there. At least, not yet.

He'd finish the case and see how she felt. He wanted her to want him, not to be beholden.

A noise sounded from inside, and he stepped back into the house, alert. The front door was locked. Everything in place.

But the noise had come from the bedroom. A crash? Voice?

He pulled his gun and ran down the hall toward the bedroom.

Chapter Twenty-One

Val was calling her name. Screaming for help.

Peyton stood at the edge of the woods, scanning the area for her sister. Sometimes Val liked to play games. Hide and seek. Where was she now?

A noise toward the west sounded, and Peyton stumbled in the bushes toward it. Her foot caught on a vine, and she fell in a tangle of weeds and briars. The prickly points stabbed her skin. The scent of a dead animal wafted toward her, and she pushed to her hands and knees. It was so dark she couldn't see two feet in front of her. So cold that her skin was chilled, and her breath puffed out in a white cloud in front of her face.

Eyes peered at her from the darkness. Followed her as she pivoted.

"Val?"

"Help me!" Val cried.

To the left, up the hill, over Copperhead Ridge where all the snakes liked to hibernate. Were they asleep now or waiting to bite?

Mama's voice—"Take care of Val. Keep her safe."

But she hadn't. Val had gotten lost.

Peyton jogged up the hill, calves clenching. A stitch splintered her side, and she massaged it with her hand.

Had to keep going. Bring Val back before Mama realized she was gone.

Limbs and twigs clawed at her. She tripped over a tree stump and scraped her hand as she reached out for something to hold on to. A branch slapped her in the face.

She shoved it away, kicked at the weeds. Her sneakers snapped twigs as she trampled them.

The stench of something dead hit her. She pressed a hand over her mouth and nose and forged on. Seconds later, Val's scream pierced the air. Peyton increased her pace, ignoring the sting of branches as they caught her in the face. Around the corner, past the pines.

She tripped again and hit the ground. Her hands slid into something sticky. Blood.

She screamed and lifted her fingers. *Oh, God, not Val.*

No...a dead deer. She struggled to her feet, maneuvered around the animal and hurried toward the ridge.

"Help me, Peyton. Help me!"

She reached the ridge and screeched to a halt, searching left and all around the woods. Trees swayed in the wind. Flies buzzed. Then she spotted her sister's hands, clawing at the ground at the edge of the ridge. She'd fallen over.

Chest seizing with terror, she raced to the ridge, dropped to her knees and reached for her sister. But she was too late. Val's hands slipped, and she lost her hold. Rocks crumbled. Dust rose from the earth. Val screamed as her body flew downward toward the ravine.

Peyton cried out Val's name, sobbing at the sight of her sister plunging below to her death.

"Peyton?"

Two hands grabbed her and yanked her up. Saved her from falling over the ridge herself.

"Peyton, wake up, it's Liam."

Liam? Not Val?

She blinked, confused and disoriented. Then she looked up into Liam's serious dark eyes.

"Nightmare," he said softly.

She choked back a sob and curled against him.

When her sister had first run away, she'd had nightmares almost every night. The guilt had nearly destroyed her. She was the big sister. Supposed to take care of Val.

Keep her safe, Mama said.

But she'd failed.

And when she'd come begging for help, she'd turned away from her.

If Val was in danger, she couldn't ignore her again.

LIAM STROKED PEYTON'S ARMS in a soothing gesture. "You were yelling the name Val," he said. "Val was your sister, right?"

Her body tensed, and she blinked as if confused. "Yes, but she's gone."

Grief tinged her voice.

"Do you want to talk about it?"

She shook her head. "No."

Liam had the strange sense she was holding something back again.

He tilted her head up, so she looked into his eyes. "If you change your mind, I'm here, Peyton. I just want to help."

Her gaze locked with his, emotions blending with the same feminine need he'd seen earlier that night.

"Then make love to me," she whispered. "Help me forget about what's going on. At least for a while."

Liam made a low pained sound in his throat. "Peyton, we talked about this. I don't want you to hate me tomorrow or have regrets."

"I won't hate you," she whispered. "And the only regret I would have is if you turned me down again."

A debate warred in his mind—his conscience, rational thought, all the reasons he shouldn't touch her and give in to desire. But the hunger in her expression triggered his own, and rational thought lost out.

She cradled his face in her hands. Tentative, then bolder, her tongue teased at his lips. Pure raw hunger ripped through him, and he gave in to temptation and kissed her deeply. She tasted like the sweetest, finest wine—delicate yet bold, and so savory that he craved another drink.

Their tongues mated and danced in a sensual game that ignited his blood with lust. A flick of his tongue along her ear and down her neck made her moan, and she pulled at the buttons on his shirt again. This time, he helped her, freeing them and tossing his shirt onto the floor.

She pushed aside the quilt on her bed and made room for him, and he crawled in beside her and cupped her breast in his hand. Her nipple stiffened, and she parted her lips on a soft, sensual sigh.

"Tell me if you want me to stop," he whispered as he lowered his mouth and teased her nipple through her tank top.

"Don't stop," she pleaded. "Please."

How could he deny her request? He wanted her, naked and hot beneath him. He wanted to be inside her. He wanted to make her cry out in pleasure instead of pain.

She stroked his calf with her foot, and he lifted her tank top and pulled it over her head. Her bare breasts were ripe and full, her nipples begging for his mouth. He gave them what they needed, sweet tongue licks and teasing, then he tugged one into his mouth and suckled her.

She lifted her hips and groaned, then pulled at his belt. He teased her other breast, pausing only long enough to yank off his belt and pants. Her pajama pants came next, gliding down her slender legs and over her round hips. They fell to the floor in a puddle with the rest of his clothes, and he dropped kisses down her abdomen to the waist of her lacy panties.

He teased her heat through the thin lace with his fingers while he suckled her breasts again. She whispered his name and clawed at his back, urging him to continue with soft moans of delight.

Slowly he lowered the lacy garment and she slipped it off, then she pushed at his boxer briefs. His sex was hard, throbbing and aching for her warm body, and when she freed him with her hand and stroked his length, he thought he might explode with pleasure.

She gripped his hips and pulled him to her, but he hesitated, then snagged a condom from his pants' pocket. A smile tilted her mouth as she helped him roll it on, then he nudged her legs apart, climbed on top of her and stroked her inner thighs with his rigid length.

Their movements became frantic as she kissed him again and wrapped her legs around his hips. He suckled at her neck, then thrust his sex into her wet heat. She groaned and lifted her hips so he could move deeper. His breath panted out as they built a steady sensual rhythm. She met him thrust for thrust, moan for moan as their slick bodies glided together.

She groaned, then flipped him onto his back and straddled him. Need and passion rose to a crescendo as her breasts swayed and she rode him harder and faster. He called her name and twisted her nipples between his fingers, then she threw her head back and cried out her release.

The raw pleasure on her face made his orgasm come swift and hard, and his body jerked as the sensations splintered through him.

PLEASURE ROCKED THROUGH PEYTON in a mind-numbing array of colors. Her chest squeezed with emotions for the strong, sexy man who'd just made love to her, and she dropped her head against his chest on a sigh.

Their sweat-slick bodies melded together as he cradled her against him and rubbed her back. "You okay?" he asked softly.

"Good. Real good," she whispered.

He chuckled. "That was amazing."

More than amazing. She feared she'd given him more than her body. She'd given him her heart. But admitting that would probably send him running.

"I'll be right back." He slipped from bed, went into the bathroom and returned a minute later. She reached for her tank and pajama pants, but he shook his head. "I like your skin against mine."

His husky voice brought a blush to her face, and she raked her hand over his bare chest. "I like it, too."

Heat flared in his eyes, and he kissed her again, then pulled her up against him and wrapped his arms around her. For the first time in forever, she curled into a man and allowed him to comfort her as she drifted back to sleep.

Hours later, as the first strains of daylight seeped through the window, she stirred and rolled over to find Liam watching her.

She smiled. "No regrets and I don't hate you," she whispered. "Do you hate me? Have regrets?"

He chuckled. "How can I hate you for giving me the best night of my life?" His voice turned husky again. "And my only regret is that we can't stay in bed like this all day."

Her cheeks blushed. She wished the same thing. But daylight brought reality. Her mother was in a coma, fighting for her life. Val was in trouble and needed her.

And someone wanted her dead.

"I keep a duffel bag with a change of clothes in my car," Liam said. "Do you mind if I use your shower?"

"Of course not. I'll start some coffee, then shower after you."

She snagged a pair of sweats from the chair in the corner, pulled them on, then headed to the kitchen. While he retrieved his duffel bag, she filled the coffee carafe with water and coffee and pressed Start.

She waited until he was in the shower, then stuffed her feet into her sneakers and left the apartment. She jogged up the hill and across the property toward the gardens. Birds chirped and twittered their morning songs, and the wind lifted dried leaves from the ground and sent them swirling across the land. More storm clouds filled the horizon, rolling across the sky in a blurry gray.

She scanned the property as she passed the central building housing the patio. Grateful the residents hadn't yet ventured outside, she wove through the rows of flowers to the rose garden.

Anxious to find whatever her sister left before Liam realized she was gone, she dropped to her knees and raked her hand along the ground beneath the bench. A second later, her finger brushed over a slight section where the ground was raised in a small mound.

Val had buried something here. She'd always liked scavenger hunts and enjoyed hiding things from Peyton.

She used her hands to dig away the dirt and found an envelope. Fingers shaking, she ripped it open. Val had left a note.

I know what happened the night Gloria Inman died. You can't trust anyone at the Gardens. We have to meet somewhere private, off the property. I'll be in touch.

Peyton's pulse jumped. How would Val know what happened to Mrs. Inman?

LIAM DRESSED IN clean clothes, then went to tell Peyton it was her turn to shower.

Time to get back to work.

The odor of strong coffee wafted toward him, and he found a pot brewed in the kitchen. Peyton wasn't in the room though, or the living area. The sound of the sliding glass doors opening echoed from the doorway, and he glanced up to see her entering.

He went still, alarm bells clanging in his head. "Where have you been?"

She lifted her brows at his tone, and he realized he'd sounded harsher than he intended. Maybe even a little possessive.

He couldn't help himself. He was damn worried about her.

"I went for a short run," she said. "I usually jog in the morning and thought it would help with my anxiety." She rolled her shoulders as if to prove her point.

"It's dangerous for you to be alone," he said. "I thought you understood that. That's the reason I stayed last night."

Hurt flickered in her eyes. "I know that. But it was just a short run and it's daylight."

He gritted his teeth as she crossed the room, removed two mugs from the cabinet and poured them both coffee. "Don't do it again," he said, softening his tone. "I don't want you to go out alone until we solve this case and make an arrest."

She stirred honey into her coffee. "Yes, sir."

He took a deep breath. "I mean it. You have to listen to me, Peyton, or I can't do my job. You're in danger."

"I know that." Her gaze met his, a myriad of emotions flashing across her face. Last night he'd made love to her, had felt close to her.

This morning she seemed distant. As if she was erecting walls.

"I'm going to shower." Spinning away from him, she took her coffee and disappeared into the bedroom.

He heard the shower water kick on and felt as if he'd just made a big mistake with her. But he didn't have a clue as to what he'd done wrong. He just wanted to protect her, dammit.

His phone buzzed. The ME, Dr. Hammerhead. "Agent Maverick."

"I have the autopsy report on Leon Brittles. Cause of death was cardiac arrest due to an opioid overdose."

Similar to Gloria Inman. "Did he have a history of taking opioids?"

"No evidence that he did from the autopsy," Dr. Hammerhead said. "And the only medication listed on his medical records was blood pressure medication."

"Did you pinpoint the drug that killed him?"

"Heroin," the ME said. "And more than four times the amount a first timer would use."

Which meant Leon Brittles had been murdered.

Chapter Twenty-Two

Liam drummed his fingers on his thigh. What motive would anyone have to kill a man in his late seventies?

Did Leon Brittles have money?

Liam ended the call, pressed Bennett's number and relayed his conversation with the ME. "Did you check Mr. Brittles's financials?"

"I did. He had no family, but it appears he had a life insurance policy that he signed over to a third party. I'm trying to track down the recipient of that policy now."

A possible theory formed in Liam's mind. "How about the three patients who died where Conrad worked? Did any of them have policies they signed over to a third party?"

"I'll look into it," Bennett said. "I've been running background checks on the list of employees at Golden Gardens and found something interesting about the director, Richard Jameson. Did you know he worked at Whistler Hospital for a while?"

"No, in what capacity?"

"He was an internist," Bennett said. "But before med school, he worked as a med tech at a pain clinic. This is where it gets interesting."

Liam sipped his coffee, impatient now. "Go on."

"He was suspended when opioids went missing. But with no proof, the clinic didn't press charges. Jameson agreed not to file a lawsuit for slander if they didn't report the issue and kept it off his record."

"Then he attended med school and now he has a script pad," Liam said. "All the access he needs for drugs for himself or to kill someone if he wanted."

"Exactly. I did some digging at the med school and while some of the instructors and docs liked him, a couple stated they had personality conflicts with him. Nothing specific about drugs. Just that his ethics were shaky."

The bedroom door opened, and Peyton emerged, looking fresh faced and gorgeous with her long wavy hair pulled back in a ponytail. Her gaze met his for a moment, and something hot and needy flared between them before she glanced away.

"Let's dig around for a motive for the director," Liam said. "Did you find anything on the names of the prescribers listed on Mrs. Inman's pills?"

"Working on them."

"Keep me posted." Bennett agreed he would, and they ended the call.

"What was that about the director?" Peyton asked.

He filled her in. "Did you know Richard Jameson worked at Whistler Hospital five years ago?"

Peyton set her coffee cup on the counter. "Yes. After the fire when the hospital had to close temporarily, and I was looking for a place to move Mama, I learned about Golden Gardens. He'd taken a job there as director." She swallowed hard. "He helped me get my job."

Every nerve cell in Liam's body jumped to alert. Had

he helped her so he could keep an eye on her because he was involved in what happened at Whistler Hospital?

PEYTON SIPPED HER COFFEE as she contemplated Liam's statement.

"Director Jameson helped you land a job here," he said.

She nodded, although his suspicious tone made her reevaluate the past. Gloria Inman's death. The threat. The fire. Her move. Her mother's near death.

Director Jameson had been in all those places. But he hadn't been in the ER the night Gloria Inman died. And he had no motive to kill her or set the fire.

"I don't understand," she said quietly.

"Neither do I. Yet. But I will figure it out." His dark gaze skated over her, a reminder of the intimacy they'd shared the night before. And that she wanted him again.

"When I want something," he said in a husky tone, "I don't give up."

If only he wanted her.

Her heart gave a pang at the thought. The fear and danger were obviously messing with her head.

She silently reminded herself that her relationship with Liam couldn't go anywhere. That he was only working a case. And she had thrown herself at him. Practically begged him to take her to bed.

But his comment about staying to watch over her had struck a nerve. She had been independent for so long that relying on someone else made her feel vulnerable.

Liam would protect her and keep her safe. At least physically.

But he could still break her fragile heart.

KNOWING SHE HAD to focus, she snagged her coat from the rack by the door. "I need to go to the hospital."

"Let's go." He pulled his keys from his pocket and she grabbed her purse and keys to lock up. They walked outside in silence, her mind racing as she remembered different encounters with the director. He had been understanding about her situation, kind to her mother and had arranged for her to have a private cottage near the garden area so she could enjoy the view.

She'd watched him with other residents and thought he had their best interest at heart.

Could she have misread him?

"Liam, do you think Director Jameson really had something to do with all this?"

Liam shrugged as he maneuvered a turn. "I don't trust anyone at this point."

Val had said the same thing. She couldn't trust anyone.

"Jameson was accused of stealing opioids when he was a med tech. He's certainly had access to them as a physician. And both Gloria Inman and Leon Brittles died with suspicious amounts of opioids in their systems."

Peyton gasped. "Leon had opioids in his system?"

"Yes, heroin," Liam answered. "But no evidence of abuse."

Peyton's eyes pinched into a frown. "Leon didn't do drugs. He hated that he had to take blood pressure medication."

"He was murdered," Liam said.

Emotions churned inside Peyton.

The suggestion that opioids might be at the crux of

the situation surrounding the hospital and suspicious deaths reminded her of Val again.

She checked her phone for a message from her sister as Liam parked at the hospital and they climbed from his vehicle.

Where was Val now?

LIAM STOOD OUTSIDE Mrs. Weiss's door as Peyton rushed in to see her. There had been no change in her mother's condition. Peyton looked forlorn as she seated herself beside her mother, stroked her hand and spoke softly to her.

His phone buzzed. Jacob. He connected. "Hey, brother."

"Morning. We found the vehicle that hit Peyton," Jacob said. "It was an older black SUV, left in an abandoned field about twenty miles north of Whistler. I've had it towed in for processing, but the paint samples match what we found on Peyton's car."

"Who owns it?"

"That's the interesting part," Jacob said. "Originally it was registered to Lydia Corgin. No record of it being sold after her death or a change of name on the title. So, either it was stolen, or someone who knew her took the car."

"Did she leave the car to someone in her will?" Liam asked.

"I didn't find a record of a will."

Liam mulled over that fact. "But if she signed her life insurance over to a third party, that party could have taken the vehicle."

"True."

"Keep at it. Hopefully we'll get prints or forensics inside the car to tell us who was behind the wheel."

He hung up, then joined the deputy who was seated outside Mrs. Weiss's door in front of the hallway computer station.

"Anything happening here?" Liam asked Deputy Rowan.

The deputy shook his head. "Just the medical staff checking vitals, that sort of thing."

"You haven't seen Brantley or Conrad?"

"No," he answered. "The director of Golden Gardens came by early this morning," Deputy Rowan said. "He showed me his ID, said he was just checking on Mrs. Weiss, that he had a soft spot for her."

Liam's breath tightened in his chest. "Director Jameson was here?"

"Yeah." The deputy frowned. "Is that a problem?"

"It might be." Liam debated whether or not to voice his concerns to Peyton. Instead he motioned for the head nurse to step into the alcove with him.

"I need you to run a full blood panel and tox screen on Mrs. Weiss."

"Is something wrong?"

"I can't explain at the moment, but it's important we verify the medication Mrs. Weiss has been given and compare with doctor's orders."

The woman's eyes widened. "I'll talk to the doctor ASAP." She pulled her phone from her belt, called the attending in charge and relayed his request. When she ended the call, she gave a nod. "I'll take the blood samples now."

He caught her arm before she went into the room. "For now, don't mention this to Peyton."

Confusion marred the woman's face. "She asked for the same thing yesterday."

Surprise hit Liam. Then again, Peyton was smart and educated. She might be putting the pieces together in the same order he was.

"Do you still want me to run it?"

"Yes." Mrs. Weiss could have been given something off the books in the past twenty-four hours. The fact that Director Jameson had been here after they'd spoken raised Liam's suspicions. Although he still didn't see how Mrs. Weiss was a threat to anyone. And if someone had hurt her because of Peyton, they'd made their point.

There was no reason to kill her.

The nurse hurried to draw blood and Jacob sent a text.

Traced Mrs. Inman's scripts to a pill mill. I'm going to check it out.

Liam sent a return text. Swing by here, and I'll go with you.

Liam hurried to tell Peyton and found her dabbing a damp cloth on her mother's forehead. "We might have a lead," he told her. "I'm going with Jacob to check it out. But you have to promise to stay here under the deputy's watch."

Emotions glittered in Peyton's eyes. "I'll be here with Mama."

He brushed her cheek with his thumb. "I mean it, Peyton. Don't go anywhere. The deputy is outside the door. He'll keep you and your mother safe until I return."

The temptation to kiss her seized him. But that would have to wait.

First, he had to find a killer.

PEYTON WATCHED LIAM LEAVE with a seed of longing. The night before, his touch, his kiss, his tenderness had awakened desires that had been dormant for too long.

Desires she had no business thinking about with her mother on her deathbed.

Shaking herself back to reality, she squeezed her mother's frail hand. "Mama, you have to keep fighting," Peyton murmured. "It won't be long until Thanksgiving. I was thinking I'll make the sweet-potato casserole you like so much with the crumb topping. And if you're up to it, you can make your homemade dressing and gravy. And how about an apple pie? It's apple-picking season now. When you wake up, we can drive to the apple orchards and pick a bushel to make the pie with." Her mother loved choosing from the selection of homemade jams and jellies, apple butter and apple bread sold at the stands on the property.

Memories flooded Peyton. "Remember when Val and I were little and you took us to the orchard, and they had that petting farm and the pig races." On the weekends, the orchard hosted u-pick apple festivals, cow milking, wagon rides, mini golf, museums, an apple-tree maze and playgrounds. Once Val had gotten lost in the maze, and it had taken Peyton almost an hour to find her and lead her out.

Her phone dinged. She startled, her pulse clamoring as she read the text.

Meet me at the goat man's house. And come alone. No cops. Remember, you can't trust anyone. Val.

An image of the wiry little man with the white beard that hung down his chest flashed in Peyton's mind. People in the mountains said he wandered the hills with his entourage of goats, living like a nomad. Sometimes, he appeared at the festivals and let the children pet the goats.

One day she and Val followed him to an old shack near the gorge. After that, they dubbed the shanty as the goat man's house.

She sent a return text. Will come ASAP.

Although a seed of doubt crept in. How had Val gotten her phone number? Could she be walking into a trap?

Deciding she had to go anyway, that no one but she and Val knew about the goat man's house, she snatched her purse, kissed her mother's cheek and whispered that she was going to find her sister. Then she stepped into the hallway.

"Restroom," she said when the deputy looked up.

He acknowledged her with a small nod, then she hurried down the hallway. She glanced back at him as she neared the corner, but he was facing her mother's doorway, so she darted past the ladies' room and into the elevator.

Knowing she needed a car, she called an Uber driver, then had him drive her to the rental-car business in town that was attached to the local garage. Twenty minutes later, she wove into the hills toward the goat man's house, checking over her shoulder as she drove to make sure no one was following her.

Dark clouds rumbled, and rain began to drizzle down. A fog spread over the ridges, the gray skies dreary, adding to her frayed nerves. She switched on her wipers and the defroster, then the radio to listen to the weather. "Temperatures are supposed to drop into the low forties tonight," the weatherman said. "With heavy rain at times, road conditions could get dangerous and flooding may occur in the lower areas of the valley."

Her tires skidded, and Peyton slowed as she rounded a sharp curve. The next mile went uphill, the drop off the shoulder of the road at least seventy-five feet. She clenched the steering wheel with clammy hands, careful not to cross the center line as she maneuvered the switchbacks. Occasionally she passed another vehicle, but the area seemed deserted, not one of the usual tourist spots.

Three more miles, and the old shanty slipped into view. Rain slackened, but the wind battered the SUV, forcing her to work to keep it on the graveled road as she climbed toward the house. A dismal gray bathed the property and shanty as she made it over the hill, and she spotted a makeshift carport covered in brush. If Val had parked here, she'd probably hidden the car beneath those limbs. Her tires chugged over the muddy ground, gravel spewing as she parked to the side of the house. She tugged her jacket on, then climbed out. Using the flashlight on her phone, she crept toward the carport.

Twigs snapped beneath her boots, and the wind hurled leaves around her. She pulled a branch aside and found an old rusted pickup. She was just about to turn and go to the house when a sound behind her made her freeze.

"Val?"

"Run, Peyton, run!"

Suddenly she felt the point of something sharp and hard in her back. A gun. Then another voice, menacing and cold.

"You should have kept your mouth shut. Now you both have to die."

Chapter Twenty-Three

The old building looked vacant. Liam and Jacob approached slowly, guns drawn in anticipation that they were about to stumble on trouble. They divided up, Liam going right and Jacob inching around the left of the building so they could see through the windows.

The windowpane was broken, so Liam hoisted himself up and peered inside. Nothing. Just an empty room.

Jacob strode toward him, boots crunching gravel. "Appears to be vacant."

"Let's search it." Liam strode to the back door, found it unlocked and went inside. As they entered, they did a quick walk-though. The building consisted of a front room, four smaller rooms, and another room in the back.

"I'll take the front room. It was probably the reception area," Jacob offered.

"I'll start in the back, in what must have been the doc's office." Jacob's boots clicked on the tile floors as he walked through the hall, and Liam yanked on gloves, then checked the desk against the wall. Except for a few pushpins and paper clips, the drawers were empty. He looked in the file cabinet, but it had been cleaned out, as well.

A piece of paper on the floor behind the desk caught

his eye, and he stooped to pick it up. A phone number was scribbled on the sticky note. He pulled out his phone and called the number, but received a recording saying the number was no longer in service.

Satisfied nothing else was in the office, he moved to one of the four exam rooms. The counter along the wall that had probably held medical supplies was bare, so he checked the cabinet. A few sterile wipes. Nothing else.

Dammit.

He moved to the second room but found nothing helpful in it either. In room three, he searched the drawers. Inside the bottom one, he spotted a prescription pad stuck in the corner. He tugged it free.

Jacob was exiting the fourth exam room. "Did you find anything?"

Liam showed him the pad.

"That's the name of the prescriber on one of Gloria Inman's prescription bottles."

"So she was getting her pills from a pill mill," Liam said. "But why kill her?"

"Maybe she planned to expose the operation," Jacob suggested.

That was a possibility.

Liam's phone buzzed. Bennett. "You asked me to dig more into Director Jameson," Bennett said. "I may have found something."

"What?"

"Your instincts were right. Edna Fouts, Lydia Corgin and Hilda Rogers all signed over their life insurance policies in exchange for medical care."

"Signed over to whom?"

"The money went into an account under the name of Benjamin Richards," Bennett said. "One contact said he paid for free care for the patients and only took the policies to pay him back, that he did it out of the goodness of his heart."

Liam cursed. Out of the goodness of his heart? The damn bastard was taking advantage of residents/patients because they had no family and was scamming the seniors out of their insurance policies.

"Did you locate this Benjamin Richards?" Liam asked.

"I did. His real name is Richard Jameson."

Liam's blood turned cold. "The director of Golden Gardens."

"He was at Whistler the night Gloria Inman died, and the night of the fire," Bennett said. "He gave Peyton her job. And now Leon Brittles died under his watch, and Mrs. Weiss is fighting for her life." Liam snapped his fingers. "Get me a warrant for his arrest. This bastard is not going to get away with hurting anyone else."

PEYTON FROZE, the gun stabbing in her back. The voice... Oh, God, she recognized it.

Joanna. Her coworker. Her friend.

You can't trust anyone there, Val had said. But Peyton had never considered the fact that her closest friend would harm her or her mother.

"Move," Joanna ordered. "Inside the shanty."

Val clutched at her arm, and Peyton realized her hands were bound together with rope. "Peyton, I'm so sorry," Val said in a shaky voice. "I never meant for any of this to happen."

Peyton stumbled as she was pushed through the back door of the rotting old house. The stench of mold and a dead animal suffused her and made bile rise to her throat.

"In the bedroom," Joanna ordered. "The corner."

Peyton couldn't hide the shock from her tone. "Why are you doing this, Jo? We were friends."

A bitter laugh rumbled from Joanna. "All you had to do was leave things alone," Joanna snapped. "Keep quiet. Not talk to the police."

"I did keep quiet." Anger bubbled inside Peyton. "Until someone hurt Mama." She glared at Joanna in shocked disbelief. "You? You caused the gas leak. And you drugged Mama. I left you with her because I trusted you, and she hasn't woken up because you drugged her."

"That was your fault," Joanna said. "You had to get chummy with that federal agent."

"I wasn't chummy," Peyton said. "I was just trying to protect my mother." She glanced at her sister who was shivering uncontrollably. Sweat beaded her skin and her eyes looked wild, glassy.

Was she high now? In need of a fix?

She rubbed her sister's arm. "Val, how did you find out what happened?"

"The pills. I couldn't help it, Peyton. I was desperate and I found this pill mill and at first it was all fine. The doc wrote me scripts, and I was okay. Then it got to where I couldn't pay, and they cut me off." Her voice slurred. "They did the same thing to Gloria. She didn't want her husband to find out she was an addict."

Peyton's mind raced as she tried to follow Val's explanation. "You knew Gloria Inman?"

"We met at the clinic. But when we couldn't pay, they told us not to come back. Gloria was irate. Said she'd expose them if they didn't give us what we needed."

Joanna waved the gun around. "We couldn't let her do that. It would have ruined everything."

Rage at Joanna heated Peyton's blood. "So, you killed Gloria. You shot her up with morphine and she OD'd. That's what sent her into cardiac arrest."

"Yeah, but her husband came in and had to call an ambulance," Joanna said in a low whisper.

A deep feeling of betrayal cut through Peyton. "At the hospital, you gave her more morphine."

"I couldn't let her wake up and point the finger at me."

"So, you framed me." Peyton's voice shook with anger. "You used my code to check out morphine and a second epi injection to make it look like I screwed up. You made Dr. Butler believe it was my fault."

Joanna gave a sardonic laugh. "He didn't want to believe it. Not that the great Nurse Weiss could make a mistake. That's why he told you not to say anything. He wanted to protect you."

"He was innocent in all this," Peyton said. But she'd doubted him.

She'd never doubted Joanna though. That was her mistake. She'd trusted the wrong person.

And now her entire family was going to die because of it.

LIAM'S PHONE BUZZED as Jacob drove them back toward Whistler. Deputy Rowan.

He connected. "Something wrong, Deputy?"

"I'm supposed to be keeping an eye out for Peyton as well as her mother, right?"

"Absolutely. What's wrong?"

"Well, Peyton came out of the room and said she was

going to the ladies' room, but that was half an hour ago and she hasn't returned."

Liam clenched the phone tighter. "Did you check the ladies' room?"

"Yeah, I knocked and called out, then asked one of the other nurses to look inside, but she wasn't there. I tried calling her phone, too, but she's not answering."

The hair on the back of Liam's neck bristled. Maybe she'd gone to the cafeteria for a bite to eat. Or to the chapel to pray. "Ask the nurse to page her over the intercom. If she doesn't show, let me know. I'll wait while you do."

He heard the deputy yell out to the nurse, then he returned. "That nurse wants to talk to you. Said she has the results of the drug screening you asked for."

"Put her on the phone."

She identified herself immediately. "The doctor reviewed the results of the screening, and something is definitely off. Mrs. Weiss was given heavy doses of morphine. But we did not have her scheduled for morphine."

Liam's breath rasped out. They had vetted every caregiver who was allowed to be in the room with Mrs. Weiss. And that was three. Director Jameson had also been there. "Did anyone else visit Mrs. Weiss other than Peyton or the three staff members on our approved list?"

"Just Peyton's friend Joanna. She was here late last night and early this morning."

"Listen to me," Liam said, his gut knotting. "Do not let anyone, including Joanna or Director Jameson in to see Mrs. Weiss. Do you understand?"

"Yes, and I can assure you that we'll monitor her medication extremely closely."

"Did Peyton answer the page?" Liam asked.

"No, and I tried her cell, but it rolled straight to voice mail."

Liam thanked her, then relayed the latest to Jacob, and pressed Bennett's number. He didn't like where his thoughts were headed. "See what you can find on Peyton's friend Joanna. She works at Golden Gardens."

"Give me a minute. I'll text you with my findings."

Liam hung up, then turned to Jacob. "Drop me at the hospital and I'll look for Peyton. Go ahead and pick up Director Jameson."

"Got it." Jacob flipped on his siren and sped toward the hospital.

Bennett's text came through: Joanna Horton looks clean. Worked at Whistler at time of Gloria Inman's death and the fire. One son, fourteen, has severe mental and physical disabilities. Lives in a group home that's expensive.

Meaning she could have been motivated by money.

Bennett: Found a photograph of her and Director Jameson on social media at a fund-raiser. Appears they're an item.

Then they could be working together.

Liam sent a return text. Peyton may be missing. Ping her phone for me and let me know her location.

On it.

Jacob reached the hospital and pulled in front of the ER entrance. "When you bring Jameson in, ask him about his relationship with Joanna. She might be involved in this."

"Copy that."

Liam jumped out and paced in front of the hospital. A minute later, Bennett sent another text.

Tracked her phone to a place in the hills. GPS coordinates following.

Cold fear swept over Liam, and he jogged toward his car. Why the hell had she gone off alone? She'd promised she'd stay put until he returned.

What if the killer had her?

"You hit my car and ran me off the road," Peyton said.

Joanna shook her head. "No, that was Herbert. He had to protect the operation."

"What operation? A pill mill?" Peyton asked.

"It's more than that," Val cut in. "They're stealing people's life insurance policies, promising to give free care to the seniors at the Gardens in exchange for becoming the beneficiary. They did it at another center before."

Peyton stared at her sister in shock. "How do you know this?"

"I heard them talking about it," Val said. "That's why I came to see Mama and you. I wanted to warn you. Make sure they didn't do that to Mama."

Peyton's head spun with the implications.

Val pulled at her arm. "I'm clean now, Peyton. It's only been nine months, but I'm working at it this time. When I saw what they were doing, I knew I had to tell you. But I knew you wouldn't talk to me if I was high."

The night Val had come to her—she hadn't attacked her. Hadn't been high.

"I didn't mean to hurt you that night," Val said. "I was just trying to stop you from running away from me so you'd listen."

Peyton's chest squeezed with emotions. Her sister had gotten clean. She sounded more like her old self. Had she found her again only to lose her?

Peyton pulled Val close as she looked up at Joanna. "Why, Jo? I thought you cared about the patients. About me. How did you get involved in drugs and cheating people out of their money? And murder?"

Anger darted through Joanna's eyes. "Those people couldn't afford the healthcare they needed. We helped them and gave them free care."

"Until you killed them," Peyton cried.

"They were old, in pain. I didn't want to see them suffer."

"Gloria Inman wasn't old or on her deathbed," Peyton said.

"She was a drug addict," Joanna pointed out. "She lied to her family and stole to pay for drugs."

"Because you kept her addicted," Peyton cried. "How could you, Jo?"

"It just got out of hand," Joanna said. "At first it was just the pills. I needed the money to take care of my son. He's disabled, you know that. And his father ran off and left us."

"If you'd told me you needed money, I would have tried to help," Peyton cried.

"You couldn't. Don't you see? The care he needs is astronomical." Joanna's voice cracked. "And by then I was already in too deep."

Peyton had to stall, somehow reach Joanna. "Do you think your son would want you to kill innocent people?"

"Leave him out of this," Joanna growled. She aimed the gun at Peyton with a shaky hand. "I didn't want to do it, but you made me. Now get in the closet."

Peyton was tempted to launch herself at Joanna, but if the gun went off, she might get Val killed.

"Please don't do this, Jo," she pleaded. "We'll figure something out. No one else has to get hurt."

"It's too late. I have no choice." Joanna's voice warbled. With a jerky movement, she jabbed the barrel of the gun in Peyton's chest. "Go. Now."

She and Val huddled together and inched into the small room. Before she closed the door, Joanna pulled a hypodermic from her pocket and jabbed Val with it. Val staggered back and slid to the floor in a puddle.

Then she pulled another needle from her pocket to inject Peyton. If Peyton allowed her to drug her, she'd never be able to save her sister. Rage fueled her strength, and she threw her arm up to deflect the injection and sent the hypodermic flying across the room.

Joanna raised the butt of the gun and slammed Peyton in the face so hard her head jerked back. She clawed at the door to remain on her feet so she could fight, but another blow sent her to the floor. Then Joanna slammed the door.

Peyton fought to stay conscious as she heard the door lock into place. But her head swirled, and the darkness claimed her.

Chapter Twenty-Four

Tension knotted every cell in Liam's body as he raced toward the address Bennett had sent. Rain slashed the car, making the ground slippery and the curvy roads even more dangerous.

His phone buzzed, and he punched Connect.

"It's Bennett," his partner said. "I analyzed those tapes from the Gardens again and ran it through a program to enhance the pixels. There was a woman outside Mrs. Weiss's cottage in the early morning hours before the gas leak."

"Yeah, there was a woman."

"It was that nurse Joanna. She was skulking around, wore all dark clothing and she went in through a back window."

Liam hissed. "If she and Director Jameson are involved, they could be working together. And no one thought anything about Joanna administering drugs or watching over Mrs. Weiss." He hesitated. "I'll call Jacob and ask him to have her picked up."

He thanked his partner, hung up and called Jacob. "I'm just about to interrogate Jameson," Jacob said.

Liam relayed his suspicions about Joanna and asked him to send a deputy to bring her in for questioning.

"Copy that. Be careful, Liam."

"Always."

He swung his car onto the side road leading into the hills. Finally, the rain dwindled, but fog remained. A half mile from the location, he noticed smoke in the air, and fear mounted inside him. The fire… Peyton?

He pressed the accelerator and sped up, shooting over the graveled, rutted road and taking turns on two wheels. Smoke billowed ahead.

He punched 9-1-1 and reported the fire, barreling closer and closer until he reached the top of the hill. Trees swayed in the wind and leaves fluttered down. Dark clouds shrouded the sky and added an eerie feel to the rotting shanty.

A white sedan was parked to the side by a makeshift carport. Joanna's? Or Peyton? Had she rented a car to get here?

Pulse hammering, he slammed on the brakes and screeched to a stop. Just as he did, a dark green SUV barreled around the corner from the back of the house. The windows were tinted so he could barely make out who was inside.

But as the SUV shot past, he saw it was Joanna.

Was Peyton inside the house or the SUV?

He couldn't let her escape. He swung his vehicle sideways to block her path. Her brakes squealed, and she swerved to avoid hitting him, then tried to swing past him. But he backed up, spun around and slammed into the side of her vehicle. Metal crunched, the passenger window shattered and the SUV skidded toward a live oak. It slammed to a stop with a bang. He threw his car into Park, pulled his gun and climbed out.

Holding his gun at the ready, he inched toward the

SUV, his breath stalling in his chest. Was the driver armed?

His boots skated over the gravel, and he kept his eyes trained on the vehicle but saw no movement. He aimed his gun inside the shattered window, then peered inside.

Joanna was slumped against the airbag, unconscious. Or so it seemed.

He couldn't risk the chance that she had a weapon. Gripping his own gun, he inched around the back of the vehicle until he reached the driver's side. Slowly he opened the door, then aimed his weapon at the woman. But she wasn't moving.

He glanced in the backseat. No Peyton.

Using two fingers, he checked for a pulse. Joanna was alive, but blood dotted the side of her face. He yanked handcuffs from his coat pocket, then quickly handcuffed her to the steering wheel. Then he cut away the airbag and raked his hand over her and the seat.

A .38 Special lay to her right. He snagged it and jammed it in his pocket. Frantic, he glanced back at the shanty. Flames were starting to shoot through the front window. A siren wailed in the distance.

But he couldn't wait. Fear for Peyton drove him, and he turned and ran toward the house.

THE SCENT OF SMOKE roused Peyton from unconsciousness. Panic stabbed at her as she rolled over and felt in the dark space for her sister.

"Val?" She raked her hand across the floor and touched her sister's arm. For a brief second, terror that Val was dead seized her, and she pressed her hand over her sister's chest to see if she was breathing.

"Val, honey, please, be okay." A slight rise and fall

of her chest indicated Val was alive. But anger at Joanna churned through her. Her sister had worked hard to get clean. Joanna may have destroyed her recovery with one injection.

Don't think about that now. You have to get Val outside.

Smoke seeped through the bottom crack of the doorway. She coughed, then covered her mouth with one hand and felt the door with the other. Not hot yet. Maybe there was time.

"Val, hang in there. I'll get us out."

She jiggled the doorknob, but the door was locked tight. Hissing between her teeth, she yanked at it, but it refused to budge. She felt in her hair for a hairpin, but had nothing, so she dropped to her knees again and felt Val's thick tresses. No hairpin there either.

Desperate, she searched the pockets of Val's jacket and found the keys to the truck outside. But they didn't fit the lock.

Balling her hands into fists, she banged on the door. "Help, please, Joanna, come back! You can't leave us here." The smoke was growing thicker, clouding the room, and fire crackled and popped outside the doorway. More noise. Something crashed—wood splintering down. Glass breaking.

Terror shot through her and she stepped back, raised her foot and kicked at the door. One kick, two. Harder each time. Another kick and another. Finally, wood splintered.

Then she heard a voice shouting. A man's.

"Peyton?"

Liam?

"Where are you?" he yelled.

She banged on the door with her fists. "In here! The door's locked!"

Footsteps pounded. Smoke clogged her nose and stung her eyes. A dizzy spell overcame her, and she blinked and reached for the wall to steady herself. Outside the door, she heard a commotion.

"Stand back. We're going to knock the door down!"

Peyton stooped and pulled her sister against the wall, then pressed her back to it and held Val's head in her lap.

Something slammed into the wall. A body? Feet?

Chaos outside. Noise. Liam wasn't alone.

Wood splintered again and cracked, creating a hole in the door. Then Liam jerked it open. Smoke filled the closet, choking the air from her lungs. Footsteps pounded. Voices shouted.

"Get those hoses by the door!"

"I've got her!" Liam stepped into the doorway and reached for her. "Peyton, come on, we have to get out!" He caught her arm, but she dug her heels in.

"My sister, she's here." She pulled him into the room. "On the floor. Joanna drugged her."

"I thought she was dead," Liam said.

"I'll explain later. We have to save her!"

"Griff, over here!" Liam yelled. "I need help."

Liam pulled her from the closet, and a firefighter appeared in full gear. "Get Peyton out!" he told Liam. "I'll get the other woman."

Peyton swayed again, her eyes stinging from the smoke, heat scalding her. Flames hissed along the far wall, inching toward them. Liam curved his arm around her and guided her through the smoky interior.

They ran through patches of flames, dodging falling

debris as the fire ate the rotting wood. Seconds later, she inhaled fresh air as they raced away from the building.

"Was anyone else inside?" Liam asked.

"No, just me and Val. Joanna locked us in there. She was behind this."

Liam coaxed her beneath a live oak far away from the fire and cupped her face in his hands. "I know. She's handcuffed in her car." He pointed to the SUV. "And Jacob arrested Director Jameson."

Griff ran toward them, carrying Val in his arms. She looked ashen faced and lethargic and was limp as Griff laid her on the ground.

Peyton raced to her and dropped down beside her. "Joanna gave her morphine," she said. "She needs to go to the hospital."

Griff ran to the fire engine and retrieved an oxygen mask, then returned and strapped it over Val's face.

Another siren wailed, lights twirling as the ambulance roared up. Peyton clung to her sister's hand as the medics climbed out and hurried toward them.

Griff raced back to join his team as they worked to contain the fire. The old shanty collapsed in a fiery blaze, flames thundering as they ate the rotting wooden boards.

One medic checked on Joanna while the other stooped to take Val's vitals. "What about you, ma'am?" the medic asked Peyton. "Are you hurt?"

Her lungs strained for air as she looked back at the fire. A few minutes later, and she and Val would both have been consumed in that blaze.

"Ma'am?" the medic asked.

She exhaled. "I'm fine. Just please…don't let my sister die."

Chapter Twenty-Five

Liam was so relieved Peyton was safe that he wanted to pull her into his arms and hold her.

But she was distraught as she hovered over her sister.

A sister she hadn't told him about. In fact, she'd lied and said her sister was dead, that her mother was the only family she had.

What else had she lied about?

A second ambulance arrived to transport Joanna to the hospital. She was still unconscious and handcuffed, and he had to ride with her.

"I have to escort Joanna," he told Peyton. "You're going in the other ambulance with your sister?"

Her troubled gaze met his. "Yes. I can't leave her."

He gave a nod. Later, he wanted an explanation. For now, he had to tie things up with the case.

He climbed in the back of the second ambulance with Joanna. While the ambulance raced to the hospital, Liam phoned Jacob and filled him in.

"The fire was set to cover up hospital records and cover for Gloria Inman's death. She was going to expose the pill mill Jameson and Joanna were running."

"I can't believe our father died because of a damn pill mill," Jacob said.

"It wasn't a small operation," Liam said. "Jameson and Joanna were also stealing patients' life insurance policies, as well."

"Jameson gave up Herbert Brantley. Said he drove the car that hit Peyton," Jacob said. "He was in it up to his eyeballs. And he's the one who actually set the fire."

"He's going to rot in jail," Liam muttered.

"Yes, he will."

"What about Conrad?" Liam asked.

"According to Jameson, Miller Conrad had nothing to do with the deaths. Joanna gave the victims the lethal injections."

"Dr. Butler was innocent, too," Liam said.

"I guess we finally got the answers we wanted," Jacob said.

"Call Fletch and Griff and let's meet for a burger later," Liam said. Tonight, he wanted them all to be together to absorb the truth about why their father had died.

THE NEXT FEW HOURS ticked by agonizingly slowly. Peyton paced the waiting room, praying for her sister and her mother.

Miraculously though, her mother regained consciousness just about the same time her sister did. "Now the drugs are being weaned out of your mother's system, she should make a full recovery," the doctor told her.

"And Val?"

"Your sister, too." Her brows pinched together. "You can see them both if you want."

First, she slipped in to see her mother. Relief at the sight of her opened eyes nearly brought her to her knees. "Mama, I'm so glad to see you're better."

"What happened?" her mother asked.

She quickly explained that there was a gas leak, but smoothed over the story. No need to upset her mother with details now. "You're going to be fine though. You just need to rest." She was tempted to tell her about Val, but she would wait to make sure Val was dedicated to her recovery first. In her frail condition, her mother didn't need the heartbreak of seeing Val and then losing her again.

Her mother's eyes were drifting closed again, so Peyton kissed her cheek and promised she'd be back. Then she hurried to her sister's room.

Val lay against the pillow, her hair fanning out, tears in her eyes. "I'm so sorry, Peyton. I…messed up so bad."

Peyton rushed over and pulled her up against her. "You were brave to get clean yourself, and even braver to come to see me and Mama and try to save the others." She stroked Val's hair. "I'm sorry I didn't listen to you the other night."

"I don't blame you. You had your reasons. I put you and Mama through hell." Val gripped Peyton's hands in hers. "But that's all over, sis. I swear. I'm going to do whatever it takes to stay clean and make you and Mama proud again."

"I am proud of you, Val," Peyton said. "But I know it won't be easy. Especially after today."

"I can do it," Val said with conviction.

For the first time since her sister became an addict, Peyton believed that she would.

LIAM WENT TO check on Peyton before he left the hospital.

"Are you okay?" he asked gently.

She nodded. "I am now. Mama's safe. And Val is here, too."

"I thought you didn't have any other family," he said, his voice a little harder than he intended. "Why did you lie to me? Let me think she was dead?"

Pain and regret darkened her eyes. "It's complicated," Peyton said. "Val is an addict. Mama and I dealt with her addiction for years. She got in trouble, stole to support her habit, lived on the streets. The last time when she checked out of rehab, she broke into our house and tried to steal Mama's china to sell. I caught her, threw her out and told her we were done. She disappeared after that. I honestly didn't think I'd ever see her again." She paused. "For a while, I felt like she *was* dead...to me."

He supposed he could understand that.

"When she showed up at the gardens, I wouldn't listen to her," Peyton said. "If I had, we could have known the truth sooner."

"Don't blame yourself," Liam said.

"Val's trying now, and this time she stepped up to save Mama," Peyton said. "She risked her life to stop Joanna and the director. I can't abandon her."

Liam itched to reach out and touch her. Draw her into his arms. Take them back to the night they shared in bed loving each other.

But the case was over, and she needed to be with her family.

"I have to meet my brothers," he said. "We're going to explain everything to Griff and Fletch."

"I'm sorry," she said in a pained whisper. "If I'd come forward sooner or if Val had, maybe Joanna and the director wouldn't have had Herman Brantley set that fire."

"It's over now," Liam said. "Stop blaming yourself, Peyton. Just try to move on."

Like he and his brothers would.

Dammit, he wanted to say more though. To make plans with her. But what kind of future could they possibly have when she didn't trust him?

So, he said good-night, then left her to be with her family while he went to meet his brothers.

Although a heaviness weighed on him. He'd thought when he closed the case and they found his father's killer, he'd feel differently.

But the pain was still there, and so was the hollow emptiness inside him.

Four weeks later

LIAM SEATED HIMSELF on the bar stool at the High Top where he and his brothers met weekly for Burgers & Brew Night. They'd started the tradition as teenagers, except the beer had been sodas, and they had resumed the tradition after their father died.

He needed the solidarity of family, and his brothers did, too.

For four weeks now, he'd nursed his feelings for Peyton, certain they would dissipate. Instead, his need had intensified.

Fletch was telling some story about Jade rescuing a puppy they'd found on the trail. "She loves that dog like it's her kid."

So did Fletch. He acted tough, but he'd always had a soft spot for animals.

Fletch swirled his beer around in his glass. "Speaking of kids, Jade is pregnant."

A chorus of cheers erupted, and they toasted Fletch and Jade's good news.

"Reese is making noises about a baby, too," Griff said. A grin tugged at his lips. "So, we may be hopping on this baby train soon."

Liam and his brothers laughed. Times had changed. They used to discuss sports and their jobs. Now their wives and families—Jacob's stepdaughter and the impending birth of his baby—dominated the conversations.

Liam was happy for them. But their conversation simply reminded him that he was alone. And that he didn't want to be.

Jacob nudged Liam's elbow. "Why don't you just call Peyton, man?"

Liam rolled his shoulders back. "What?"

"He's right." Griff poured himself a fresh mug of beer from the pitcher on the table. "You've been miserable without her."

"I'm not miserable," Liam protested.

Jacob chuckled. "You haven't touched your burger. You don't talk. You just sit and brood."

Liam sipped his beer. "I just don't understand why she didn't trust me. She was supposed to wait for me instead of going off on her own to meet her sister. And she lied to me about having a sibling."

"Cut her some slack," Fletch said. "Look at the position she was in."

"Addicts cause all kinds of problems in families," Griff said. "Put yourself in her shoes. She was threatened, left alone to deal with a sick mother and didn't know who to trust."

But he'd wanted her to trust him.

Jacob checked his watch. "If you care about her, Liam, go tell her."

"Yeah, she can't read your mind," Fletch added.

Griff grunted. "Go get her, bro."

Liam's heart stuttered. He'd told Peyton that when he wanted something, he didn't give up. And he didn't give up on a case.

Yet he'd given up on them too easily.

His brothers were right. He'd just have to work harder to earn Peyton's trust.

He tossed some cash on the table. "You're right. I'm going to see her right now."

His brothers clinked glasses and cheered him on as he hurried out the door. Not wanting to show up empty handed, he stopped at his place and retrieved the antique ruby ring his mother had left him. It wasn't a diamond, but it would do until Peyton could pick out one. That is, if she said yes to his proposal.

Fall was in full swing as he drove toward the mountains and the Gardens, the bare branches fluttering in the gusty wind. Thanksgiving was just around the corner, a time for family.

He wanted his own family now, one with Peyton.

The temperature was dropping to near freezing tonight, but he was sweating in his shoes as he paused at the gate to Golden Gardens. Once he was buzzed through, he parked in front of Peyton's apartment, then sat for a moment, wondering if he should have called. She might be with her sister or mother. Or working.

Or, hell, she might be seeing another man by now.

That thought made his stomach twist into all kinds of knots, and he climbed out and strode up to her door. He rang the bell, jiggling his leg as he waited.

Doubts crept in. What if Peyton didn't want him in her life?

Hell, he dodged bullets and fought the dregs of society. But opening his heart was the scariest thing he'd ever done.

Too late to turn back now. He'd regret it in the morning.

Summoning his courage, he rang the bell again, but she didn't answer, so he walked around the side of the property and spotted her by the pond near the gardens. He hesitated, not wanting to disturb her if she was with someone else. But as he walked toward her, he realized she was alone. Well, except for the furry cat in her arms which she cradled close to her.

He halted a few feet from her, and she turned, her gaze locking with his. The instant flare of attraction sizzled through him, and he could barely breathe. She looked more rested and at peace than she had before.

And so beautiful he called himself ten kinds of a fool for waiting so long to confess how he felt.

He cleared his throat. "Peyton?"

She kissed the cat and set him on the ground, and he ran back toward her apartment. "I didn't think I was going to see you again," she said softly.

He moved toward her, heart pounding. "I thought you needed time." And he'd been a coward.

"I did, but Mama and Val are both doing great." The tender smile she gave him warmed him from the inside out. "I'm sorry I didn't tell you about Val. I…it just hurt so much when I thought of her."

He crossed the distance to her. "I understand. But I want you to trust me." He stood in front of her, need and desire thrumming through him.

"I do trust you, Liam. It was never about trust with you." She licked her lips. "It was just complicated. And painful."

"I know, and I'm sorry." He reached up and tucked a strand of hair behind her ear. "I haven't been able to stop thinking about you."

A slow smile creased her sensual lips. "I wanted to see you, too."

"I don't want any regrets," he said. "And if I don't tell you how I feel, I will regret it."

Emotions thundered inside him, and he reached for her. "I'm in love with you, Peyton."

She looped her arms around his neck and smiled up at him, her blue eyes sparkling. "I love you, too, Liam."

Joy burst inside him, and he closed his mouth over hers and kissed her tenderly.

When he pulled away, he dropped to his knee and lifted the velvet ring box. "It's not a diamond. I thought you'd want to pick that out. But this ring belonged to my mother. She told me to give it to the woman I wanted to spend the rest of my life with." Peyton gasped as he opened the box, tears filling her eyes.

"Will you marry me, Peyton?"

"Yes," she whispered as she stared at the sparkling red stone. "And the ring is beautiful." With a shaky hand, he removed the ring from the box and slipped it on her finger.

Passion ignited between them, and he swung her into his arms to carry her inside. He wanted to make love to her all through the night. They kissed frantically and by the time they reached her door she was tearing at his shirt.

But his phone buzzed on his hip. He froze, then cursed. Dammit, not work. Not now.

"You have to get it?" Peyton asked.

He didn't want to. But he'd better see who it was, so he set her on her feet, then pulled his phone from his pocket and glanced at the number.

A text. Jacob. Cora's in labor.

"What's wrong? Work?" Peyton asked on a ragged breath.

He shook his head. "Jacob's wife is in labor."

Her eyes twinkled, and she rebuttoned his shirt for him. "I guess you need to go then."

He kissed her again, a kiss filled with passion. "We'll finish this later." Then he offered his hand to her. "Come with me. Meet the rest of my family?" he asked gruffly.

She joined her hand with his, a deep sense of rightness spreading through him at her murmured yes. Then they hurried to his car and climbed inside.

As he sped toward the hospital, he clung to her hand, anxious to make love to her again.

But he wrangled his libido under control as he parked at the hospital. Together, they hurried inside and found Fletch, Jade, Griff and Reese in the waiting room. Cora's daughter Nina was with them, rocking her doll in her arms as the adults paced.

An hour later, Jacob burst through the door in hospital garb, a grin splitting his face. "It's a boy. We're going to name him after Dad!"

"I have a brother!" Nina ran and jumped into Jacob's arms and he spun her around, then congratulations began. Finally, when everyone had hugged and the women cried, Jacob looked at Liam and gestured toward Peyton. "Aren't you going to introduce her to the family, Liam?"

Griff and Jacob had met Peyton, but no one else had. Liam pulled her up against him and kissed her, then lifted their joined hands in a celebratory gesture. "This is Peyton Weiss, the woman I intend to marry."

She threw her arms around him, then the congratulations began again.

The hollow emptiness in Liam faded. He felt whole again. And there would definitely be more babies in the future as their family grew.

It was the start of a new era for the Mavericks.

* * * * *

Look for more books from USA TODAY bestselling author Rita Herron in 2021!

And don't miss the previous books in A Badge of Honor Mystery miniseries:

Mysterious Abduction
Left to Die
Protective Order

Available now wherever Harlequin Intrigue books are sold!

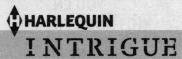
#1959 ROOKIE INSTINCTS
Tactical Crime Division: Traverse City • by Carol Ericson
TCD team member Aria Calletti is determined to find out why women are turning up dead. The newest victim's half brother, Grayson Rhodes, has sacrificed everything to find his half sister and her son. But can a civilian and a new agent take down a drug kingpin?

#1960 TEXAS TARGET
An O'Connor Family Mystery • by Barb Han
After bailing Summer Grayson, his ex-wife's identical sister, out of jail, US marshal Dawson O'Connor agrees to help Summer, who is convinced her twin is in danger. He'll do anything to protect her, even as she ups the stakes by posing as her missing sibling.

#1961 CLOSE RANGE CHRISTMAS
A Badlands Cops Novel • by Nicole Helm
Dev Wyatt's worst fear has come true. Someone from the Wyatts' dangerous past is stalking his family—and his best friend, Sarah Knight, who is pregnant with his child. As Sarah and Dev battle escalating threats, will they survive long enough to become a family?

#1962 INVESTIGATION IN BLACK CANYON
The Ranger Brigade: Rocky Mountain Manhunt
by Cindi Myers
After Cara Mead's boss disappears in the wilderness, Cara enlists the help of Ranger Brigade officer Jason Beck. But once the manhunt is set in motion, Jason and Cara find themselves embroiled in a fearsome conspiracy—and someone will do anything to keep them from finding out the truth.

#1963 DANGEROUS KNOWLEDGE
Fortress Defense • by Julie Anne Lindsey
After investigative journalist Katlin Andrews is run off the road, she awakens with Fortress Defense bodyguard Jack Hale in her hospital room. He promised to protect his best friend's sister. With Katlin unable to recall who's after her, he'll have to use all his skills to stop an unseen threat.

#1964 HIGH-PRIORITY ASSET
A Hard Core Justice Thriller • by Juno Rushdan
When US marshal Dutch Haas enters Isabel Vargas's life to get information on her uncle, he knows she'll become his partner instead of his mark. With threats stacking up, will Isabel and Dutch be able to stop Isabel's past from catching up with her before it is too late?

The wind whipped off the lake, its chilly tentacles snaking into his thin black jacket, which he gathered at the neck with one raw hand, stiff with the cold. His other hand dipped into his pocket, his fingers curling around the handle of the gun.

His eyes darted toward the dark, glassy water and the rowboat bobbing against the shore before he stepped onto the road…and behind his prey.

She hobbled ahead of him, her shoes crunching the gravel, her body tilted to one side as she gripped her heavy cargo, which swung back and forth, occasionally banging against her leg.

A baby. Nobody said nothing about a baby.

He took a few steps after her and the sound of his boots grinding into the gravel seemed to echo through the still night. He froze.

When her footsteps faltered, he veered back into the reeds and sand bordering the lake. He couldn't have her spotting him and running off. What would she do with the baby? She couldn't run carrying a car seat. He'd hauled one of those things before with his niece inside and it was no picnic, even though Mindy was just a little thing.

He crept on silent feet, covering three or four steps to her one until he was almost parallel with her. Close enough to hear her singing some Christmas lullaby. Close enough to hear that baby gurgle a response.

The chill in the air stung his nose and he wiped the back of his hand across it. He licked his chapped lips.

Nobody said nothing about a baby.

The girl stopped, her pretty voice dying out, the car seat swinging next to her, the toys hooked onto the handle swaying and clacking. She turned on the toes of her low-heeled boots and peered at the road behind her, the whites of her eyes visible in the dark.

But he wasn't on the road no more.

He stepped onto the gravel from the brush that had been concealing him. Her head jerked in his direction. Her mouth formed a surprised O, but her eyes knew.

When he leveled his weapon at her, she didn't even try to run. Her knees dipped as she placed the car seat on the ground next to her feet.

She huffed out a sigh that carried two words. "My baby."

He growled. "I ain't gonna hurt the baby."

Then he shot her through the chest.

Don't miss Rookie Instincts *by Carol Ericson,*
available November 2020 wherever
Harlequin Intrigue books and ebooks are sold.

Harlequin.com

Love Harlequin romance?

DISCOVER.

Be the first to find out about promotions,
news and exclusive content!

f Facebook.com/HarlequinBooks

🐦 Twitter.com/HarlequinBooks

📷 Instagram.com/HarlequinBooks

📌 Pinterest.com/HarlequinBooks

ReaderService.com

EXPLORE.

Sign up for the Harlequin e-newsletter and
download a free book from any series at
TryHarlequin.com

CONNECT.

Join our Harlequin community to
share your thoughts and connect
with other romance readers!
Facebook.com/groups/HarlequinConnection